HIS SEMI-C

Billionaire Breakfast Club #1

LISA HUGHEY

Lisa Hughey

HIS SEMI-CHARMED LIFE

Billionaire Breakfast Club #1
By
Lisa Hughey

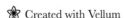 Created with Vellum

PROLOGUE

June 1997

Worst. Summer. Ever.

Diego Ramos strode out to the parking lot, ignoring the rules to go check on his precious car. His '69 Charger had gotten him here but he'd lost his muffler on the way up. He'd growled the final miles to Camp Firefly Falls on the faulty part.

He'd been working on this car forever. He was finally old enough—sort of—to drive it, even though he'd been tooling around Dot illegally for the past few years.

He was working all summer to pay for the muffler at cost. He'd been planning to buy the one Tío Raul had at his garage. But before Diego could scrape together the money, one of Raul's full-paying customers needed one and his uncle couldn't turn down the sale. Their family friend Hector said he might be able to get his hands on a replacement. Might. But if he got a full paying customer,

Hector had to sell it to them, because he needed the money too.

It was the worst to be stuck here. He totally understood that if they had buyers while he was here at camp, he was screwed. He had to stay at camp to make enough money to buy the part.

He kicked at a stone, sent it scuttling into the brush that lined the path.

A single spotlight on a post cast more shadows than illumination over the lot—which was really just a decent-sized opening between two stands of trees.

Diego opened the hood. Not a squeak. He took damn good care of his baby.

He stroked the sleek, clean engine like he was petting his little cousin's cat. "Soon, baby. You'll be all prettied up," he crooned to the engine like she was a girl.

He flushed, glanced around, but no one had seen him talking to his car like she was real.

Diego climbed up on the trunk of his car and lay back to stare up at the stars. The Charger was the one constant in his life. His mother and father were in and out. He had bounced from relative to relative until his uncle got married a few years ago and then he'd gone to live with his tío and tía permanently.

His uncle got him this camp job through one of his customers. Diego was supposed to be thankful for it. He was. Sort of. He'd never tell anyone but he missed his little cousins, Raul Jr. and Zinnia, even though they annoyed him ninety-nine percent of the time.

One thing he'd give to these mountains, the sky was

amazing. Light from the stars twinkled in deep blue mysterious space.

"What'cha doing?"

He jerked up so fast his head went dizzy.

And there she was.

He *hated* working here. Little Miss Princess Penelope embodied every single reason. She was only like nine years old and so damn smug. She'd been whining since her parents dropped her off at the beginning of the week. They were in Europe. Without her. *Boo. Fricking. Hoo.*

"You're not supposed to be out here," he snarled. Dammit. Why was she here?

Penelope Hastings stood there looking at him with those stupidly innocent, bright green eyes. "Neither are you."

"Get back to your cabin." Except he was going to have to take her. He couldn't let her wander around in the dark. Part of his job was making sure the campers were safe.

"Why are you so upset?" She stepped closer to his car.

Her pout caused everything to bubble up inside him. Couldn't he get frustrated and angry in peace? Couldn't he have one damn minute alone? Apparently not, if he wanted enough money to keep fixing up his baby.

"Let me take you back to your cabin." Diego sighed. He slid off the trunk, dropped to the dirt and gravel parking lot, then took a second to stroke his palm over the blue paint before he gently eased the hood closed.

She danced back a step. "Is something wrong with your car?"

"Yeah."

She frowned, her ginger eyebrows crinkled as if the

concept of car problems was beyond her. "Why even bother working on that old piece of junk?"

Junk? Maybe to her it was junk but to him this car was everything. It was freedom. It was life. It was his future.

"Aren't you only fifteen?"

And she was nine. They'd done the whole introduce yourself in a circle on the first day. So he knew her name was Penelope Hastings, she was rich as fuck, and so super sad that her parents had left her at camp instead of taking her to Europe.

"So?" So he'd driven here slightly illegally. So the fuck what? He had his permit.

"Well, if you're only fifteen—" She laughed, a delighted trill of sound, like the birds in the forest only softer, and weirdly sweeter. "When's your birthday?"

He trudged toward the line of cabins where the girls stayed. "September."

What that had to do with anything he had no fucking idea. Of course, he never claimed to understand rich kids. They lived in their own stupid bubble.

She clapped her soft pale hands and laughed again. "Well then, silly. You only have to wait a couple more months and you'll get your new car for your sixteenth birthday!"

She dropped the words so eagerly, so happily, as if she'd magically solved his problem and everyone in the fucking world got a car when they turned sixteen.

"That's about as likely as the Red Sox winning the World Series."

"I don't understand."

"Welcome to the real world where kids don't get new

cars on their birthdays, you spoiled brat." Shit, he was going to get in trouble for that. He was a counselor. And he needed this job so he could afford the parts for his beloved car.

Yeah, the owners made it seem like they were all equal and happy and shit, but the reality was, Diego worked for Miss Richy-Rich Hastings.

"Oh." Her face fell, her brows scrunched together as if she were actually trying to imagine a world where kids didn't get a new car when they turned sixteen. "So not everyone gets a car?"

Could this kid be any dumber?

"There's a whole world of people who don't have food to eat at night, don't wear shoes without holes." Ugh, she glanced down at his feet and his ratty old Converse. "And don't get new cars. So, no."

"That's…too bad."

"Yeah, it's a real fucking nightmare."

Her shoulders slumped. Her dark ginger hair was almost Charger Red in the soft light of the parking lot.

"Well," she said brightly, her smile reappearing. "My dad always says, 'How do we turn this failure into a success?'"

"I'm a failure? Thanks for making your opinion loud and clear."

God, he hated her. She was everything he wasn't. Clean and perfect. Her blindingly bright white tennis shoes and her naïve, always smiling face versus his threadbare high tops, soles so worn they were just about to crack, and his scowl.

Her smile faltered. "Oh no, of course not. He just says,

'When things don't go the way you planned, you work with what you've got, and turn that negative into a positive.'"

"I've got *nothing*." Diego spit out the words. He wanted, with an agonizing pain in his heart, to throw some dirt on her. To ruin that sparkly perfection so she was as dirty and grumpy and mean as he felt inside. "So get the hell out of here, you stupid little rich girl."

Tears filled her bright green eyes. She lifted her trembling chin and shot him a vengeful glare. "I was just trying to be a good friend."

"Yeah, well, I don't need any friends. Go away."

She finally ran down the path toward the cabins. He should go after her, follow her and make sure she got back to her cabin without harm. But he flung himself on the hood of the car.

He was so getting fired.

As he lay there, his initial rage simmered and stewed as he kept reviewing their conversation. And dammit, the picture she painted wouldn't leave him.

A new car for his sixteenth birthday. The promise that he'd never go cold or hungry again. The shiny idea that he could turn a failure into a success dangled out of reach like a sparkling lure on the hook of life.

He lay under the stars dreaming of that life and ignoring the reality that he was probably going to get fired. Which would mean no new part for his car, no awesome life, no perfect future.

But in the morning, a subdued, less sparkly Penelope Hastings never said a word to the camp director. She also never spoke to Diego again. He knew he should apologize. But he didn't.

6

That regret festered in his heart. Once he got back to Dorchester, he decided he could apologize next summer. But after that first summer, he'd been able to work in his uncle's garage, learning more about cars and mechanic skills. Then camp closed and he never got the chance to apologize.

But he never forgot her.

❦ I ❦

Present Day

Penny Hastings twirled in a circle, her head thrown back and her face tilted toward the cerulean sky with puffy white clouds floating above her. Laughter burst from her chest in an explosion of joy. Like a kid, she whirled until she was too dizzy to keep turning. "I'm baaackk."

Seventeen years since she'd been a camper at Camp Firefly Falls, and now happy memories flooded her.

This place was the scene of the best times of her young adolescence, and her heart overflowed with delight as her gaze touched on landmarks, the lake, the boathouse, the dock, the cabins, each spurring their own vignette of happiness.

A lot had changed.

Penny staggered over to the nearest tree and leaned against the trunk, waiting for the world to stop spinning. She might have lain down in the grass but since she hadn't yet checked in with her pal, Meg, or the owners of the newly renovated summer camp, Michael and Heather Tully, she didn't want to start off on the wrong foot with grass in her hair and dirt on her face.

Her gaze slipped to the large oak and the bumpy rutted staff parking lot mostly hidden by a row of bushes. And for a moment her happiness dimmed.

There was one memory that wasn't good, and yet, that night had changed her life.

She shoved away from the massive old oak tree and grabbed her simple canvas duffel from the back of her car. Most of the time she tooled around in her battered Ford F250 pickup. The '69 Charger was her pride and joy but she didn't get many chances to drive her.

Another souvenir from the memories of her first year at camp. That confrontation between her and Counselor Diego had impacted her in ways she'd never have foreseen when she'd been young, immature, and spoiled. Her only regret was that she'd never had the chance to tell him how he'd changed her perspective on the world.

Shaking off the odd memories, Penny headed down a path lined with cheerful wild azaleas to the beautifully restored Pinecone lodge. What a great job the Tullys had done.

Penny dropped her duffel on the porch. She couldn't remember if she'd spruced up before she left the farm this afternoon. Working in the dirt most days she barely slathered on moisturizer and sunscreen. If she was feeling particularly fancy she'd slick some Burt's Bees on her lips.

Penny did a quick inventory, took out her ponytail and threaded her fingers through her too-long hair—she really needed to get it cut again—then twisted it back up into a haphazard bun. She rubbed her palms together, checked for dirt under her fingernails—hazard of her life— and brushed her fingers over her cheeks and underneath her eyes and over her brows hoping that she didn't have any mascara smudges.

As ready as she'd ever be, Penny took a deep breath, let out it out, then knocked on the front door.

The large wood-paneled door flung open. "Penny!" Meg squealed and dragged her inside the lodge.

Penny laughed, thrilled to see Meg again. She was the one who'd gotten her this gig at Camp Firefly Falls.

"Oh my gosh, it's good to see you," Meg said. Penny and Meg both worked seven day weeks and they lived hours apart so they rarely got to see each other in person.

"I'm so sorry about the restaurant." Meg's restaurant had burned down. She was going to rebuild but since she had no place to cook right now, she'd agreed to come back to camp this summer.

"Thanks." A shadow fell over Meg's features, and she tilted her head forward, her curly brown hair hiding her features. Her bold vibrant personality dimmed for a moment. Then Meg slung her arm over Penny's shoulder, her wide smile once again brassy and welcoming. "How are *you*?"

"Excited to get started." Penny had conceived of FEED Together, the small garden and farming opportunity for corporations, as her senior thesis at UMass Amherst. Pretty Penny Farms, her small woman owned farm was finally doing well enough that she could devote some time to the philanthropic and therapeutic program that had been haunting her for a long time.

Penny planned to consult with businesses about installing small gardens on their rooftops or courtyard areas and having their employees take care of the gardens. The employees would get outside, commune with nature, and grow food—either for company consumption or as donations to local food banks.

When she and Meg had initially discussed her thesis, Penny hadn't figured a way to get the word out about the semi-radical proposal.

Then Meg had the idea to approach her bosses at Camp Firefly Falls to see if they would be open to Penny presenting her idea at one of the corporate retreats scheduled this summer.

Her program had a lot of potential. The nonprofit charter would hopefully be a win for both companies and food charities. This weekend was a test run to refine her sales pitch, and gauge how to sell the philanthropic idea to companies. She needed financial participation by the companies in order to get the idea off the ground. If she could secure some initial commitments, she could prove the concept would work.

So here Penny was. She was helping the Tullys with the corporate retreat this weekend, and in exchange, Penny got to pitch her nonprofit idea to the companies attending the retreat and set up her first garden for Camp Firefly Falls. Her thesis idea was one step closer to becoming a reality.

The scent of something burning caught Penny's attention. "Um, Meg?"

"Crap! I left the onions sauteeing." Meg ran.

Penny followed her friend toward the kitchen. "Let's just

throw in a frozen pizza," she said as Meg waved the smoke from the burned onions.

At the momentary sadness on Meg's face, Penny attempted to divert her. "Are Michael and Heather here?"

"They'll be back tonight or early tomorrow before the campers arrive to check in."

"What time is check in?"

"Starts at two," Meg said. "First bus will get here about then."

Penny laughed. "Bus?"

"Yep. The retro camp experience."

"That's great."

"There are always a few campers who are too busy or too 'important,'" Meg put air quotes around the word, "to take the bus, but most of the campers embrace the experience."

"It's a shame they aren't grateful for the chance to reconnect with nature." Penny hadn't stopped smiling since she got here.

"Yeah, well what are you going to do," Meg said. "Sometimes we resist that kick in the butt."

"Their loss." Penny didn't waste any more time thinking about reluctant campers. "Show me where we're going to set up the gardens."

❧

IT WAS SO FUCKING dark up here.

The night sky was liberally sprinkled with stars but that light didn't lend much visibility here on the ground. In the woods there were no street lights, no street signs. He was tired, cranky, and if Zinnia, his pain in the ass assistant and cousin, was here right now, he'd personally cut her salary.

Diego creatively cursed his cousin, his late departure, and the world in general.

He didn't want to be here.

His 2007 Porsche Carrera GT really didn't want to be here. At the rate he was bumping over the uneven ground, his suspension was going to need a realignment tomorrow.

The camp held nothing but bad memories. Except…his recall of the little girl who'd had a profound impact on the course of his life was complicated. Regret and gratitude all rolled together.

Some days he wondered if he would be where he was if it wasn't for little Penelope Hastings and her blind optimism. Which was why he hadn't blasted Zinnia after she booked this retreat.

Finally, Diego arrived in the clearing. The deserted clearing.

There were only two cars in the matted down grass and gravel parking lot. Then he remembered—this was the employee parking lot. There was probably a separate one for guests.

Diego pulled up next to a sweet, perfectly restored Charger. He got out of the silver metallic Porsche, ignored the empty camp and instead bent to peer at the leftover remnant of his youth. The car was an exact replica of his very first car. The one he'd lovingly restored. The impetus for one of the worst moments of his life.

The paint job was perfect, the Bright Blue Poly an original color. She also had a white racing stripe with a hint of metallic sparkle in the paint.

God, he'd loved that damn car.

In the distance the faint sound of music drifted on the still summer evening. Fireflies buzzed in the thin woods. He spied the path to the main lodge.

He tried to dredge the camp check-in details from his brain. But he'd mostly tuned Zinnia out when she'd been admonishing him not to be late.

He was late.

It wasn't exactly his fault. He'd gotten caught up in contract negotiations with his company's lawyer, and Jeffrey London, the CEO of London Automotive. They were in talks to merge London Automotive with Ramos's Classic Auto Restoration. Diego was on the brink of the culmination of twenty years of planning and ambition.

To Diego's delight, the Billionaire Breakfast Club was about to indoctrinate another member.

And he couldn't wait.

Merging was a solid business decision. Ramos's Classic Auto Restoration had gotten big. They were all working extra hard. If they merged, the company would be bigger but there'd be more people for work distribution. London's business dovetailed well with Diego's. Their combined company would seriously increase his net worth.

But as Diego cast one last longing look at that Charger, he realized he hadn't geeked out and wrenched on a car in…he couldn't even remember.

He sighed.

Tinkering with a classic car wouldn't increase his bottom line, and a gearhead wouldn't get bigger and better in a coverall with grease under his fingernails.

He grabbed the leather suitcase from the passenger seat

and headed toward the registration tent through the trees. A circular driveway was empty. The canvas structure in the middle of a grassy expanse inside the circle held a 6 x 2 foldup table and a plastic green file box closed tight. A single Papermate pen rested in the crevice between the file box and the table surface.

That was it.

He pulled out his cell phone so he could call Zin.

No service.

Diego sighed. The main lodge was down the path not too far in the distance. He'd check in there.

The single porch light cast a warm yellow glow over the painted wooden balustrade. As he walked toward the light, he searched the shadows and realized the camp seemed awfully empty and quiet.

The ground was slightly squishy. It must have rained up here sometime this week. He grimaced when he thought about the mud clinging to his Italian loafers and dampening the bottom of his silk trousers.

Diego strode up to the lodge. Muted laughter and music came through the open window. He rang the doorbell.

"Coming!"

Within in seconds, the door flew open and a woman tumbled out.

Rich auburn hair framed her sun-kissed classic bone structure. She had tanned cheeks with a smattering of freckles across her nose, a lush full mouth, and remarkable bright green eyes, the exact shade of classic Charger Rallye Green. She sparkled with amusement and happiness and an inner glow. She held a tumbler of white wine in long elegant fingers with short unpainted nails.

"Oh, hello." She straightened her plump lips, trying to contain the laughter that had graced her features when she'd opened the door.

Diego frowned. She looked…familiar. Except not. He had an excellent facility for remembering faces. That skill had served him well in business. He ran her features through his memory banks. She was there, just out of reach. As if he *should* know her.

Except for that single light, the porch was bathed in darkness.

"Ah, can I help you?" She fiddled with the tail of a man's plaid shirt over her camisole. The thin white cotton revealed small breasts with an intriguing shadow in the valley between them. Her faded loose jeans with holes in the knees were rolled up to reveal delicate ankles and toenails painted a surprising bright neon green.

Like a wolf, his body was instinctively attuned to her. Her features tripped some switch inside him, primitive and needy. His brain stuttered on those bright toes, thinking about how he'd like to start at the arch of her foot and spend hours discovering the secret hollows and erogenous places on her body, just like he learned each nook and cranny and idiosyncrasy of a 5.7-liter HEMI V-8.

"I'm here for the camp," he blurted out when he realized he'd been quiet for far too long.

"Okay." In the background, Third Eye Blind's 90s hit "Semi-Charmed Life" played. The furniture in the living area had been pushed back against the walls. A coffee table was littered with two empty plates and a mostly empty bottle of wine.

"Penny. Did I hear the doorbell?" Another woman,

brown curly hair and generous curves, skidded into the room. "Can we help you?"

"I'm here for the camp," he said again clearly, but he finally clued in to the fact that no one else was here. Just these two women.

Diego was still in his suit and tie, the offending silk noose now strangling him.

The woman who answered the door blinked. "The one that starts tomorrow?" Now she was hastily trying to shove her hair into the knot at the top of her head.

"Tomorrow," he said flatly.

Diego pulled his phone from his pocket. His lifeline. Everything was on the state of the art smartphone. He accessed his calendar. No. "According to my calendar, it was supposed to start today."

"I'm sorry—"

"Dammit." He was going to kill Zinnia.

The redhead straightened, the smile disappearing from her face. "Excuse me?"

"Not you." Diego had figured out what happened. Zin made sure he was here before camp started by giving him the wrong date. "My assistant."

He punched the button on the phone and returned it to his pocket.

"She entered the date incorrectly?"

He twisted his wrist, stared at the roman numerals on his watch, and blinked at the time. It was after ten at night. No wonder they hadn't been expecting him.

"More like an end run," he muttered. "What time tomorrow?"

"Two," the curvy brunette said.

Diego sighed. He was tired. He'd started his day at five a.m. and had been running ever since. He rubbed his hand over the stubble on his jaw and sighed. "I'll be back."

"You can't leave now." The redhead propped one foot on top of the other and leaned against the door frame. "Briarsted doesn't have any hotels. There's no place to stay nearby. Right, Meg?"

Diego certainly wasn't sleeping in his car. Those days were long over. He propped his fists on his hips, and his stomach growled. Loudly.

The grinding in his stomach that was near constant these days ramped up its slow attack on his body. Stress and hunger were not a good combo.

"There's got to be an empty room in the lodge," Penny, the auburn-haired goddess, said to the other woman. "Right?"

"Let me just turn off the music."

"Clearly, I've interrupted your…evening," Diego said politely. "I'll let you go."

At the same time, Penny said, "We were just dancing."

His gaze skimmed between the two very attractive women. "I'll let you get back to it."

"Oh! No, we're not." Penny laughed, a light trill of sound, as her eyes twinkled with a mirth. Something about that laugh triggered another flare of lust deep in his belly. "It's fine. You're fine."

"He certainly is," Meg said under her breath, but Diego heard her.

Okay. Not lovers then.

Lover. The word conjured hot nights, liquid sighs, fevered kisses…and oddly the woman who'd answered the door.

He didn't have time for a lover. But damn if his mind didn't zoom right back to the redhead when he realized the two women were only friends.

"Come on in and we'll figure out a place for you to sleep." The brunette shoved out her hand. "I'm Meg, the camp chef, and this is Penny. She's going to be running a corporate farm team-building experiment."

Diego tried to keep the grimace from his face but he must have failed because the chef laughed.

"It will be fun," Penny said defensively. "I promise."

Her gaze skimmed his silk suit, pressed shirt, and Italian tie. "Although hopefully you've got something more casual in that bag. Farming, and camping, are messy."

Her smile was wide, and her white straight teeth bit into her unpainted lip.

Meg said, "I can't check you in, no idea how that works. Let me show you a room where you can crash, Mr....?"

He was more addled than he thought. Combo of a long day and the intriguing Penny with the neon toenails and the mysterious green eyes.

"Diego Ramos." He held out his hand so he could shake hers.

He couldn't help but notice Penny's reaction. She'd jolted, her bright green eyes wide.

Did he know her?

Holy manure.

Diego Ramos was here.

Her childhood crush and the boy whose anger and resentment had opened her eyes to a whole new universe one summer. She'd come back to camp every summer until Firefly Falls closed. But she'd never again seen the counselor who'd upended her narrow view of the world.

Their encounter had been strange, upsetting, and eye-opening.

Penny had never forgotten him.

She'd gone home that summer and begun learning about the world outside her tiny bubble. Which fortunately had saved her when her sheltered, rarified existence had imploded.

In a small way, Diego Ramos had been the one who saved her.

"Penny why don't you…entertain our guest while I make up a room."

Entertain conjured images she shouldn't be thinking about. But dang, she'd like to entertain him.

Oh, bad Penny. She couldn't think that way. But as she catalogued his swarthy skin, eyes the color of a fertile soil, and a mouth made for kissing, a flush started in her core and spread outward, her body tingling with desire.

Woo, she was hot.

"Sure." Her voice came out husky. "Come on in."

He hesitated for another second on the porch as if still thinking about searching out alternative lodging.

"There really isn't anything close by."

"Thank you." He followed her inside the comfy common area of the lodge. "I am sorry to impose."

His delivery was so stiff, so formal. Uptight. Closed off.

In her memory, the boy had stayed young and angry. Because even though she'd been nine, she understood that he'd been filled with rage.

Back then she'd been hurt and confused. He probably didn't even remember her. Or their fraught confrontation.

Now she just wanted to climb him like the hundred-year oak that marked the entrance to her farm and cling onto his sexy body.

Diego Ramos had grown up fine.

A bit of stubble scattered over his chin and around his mouth, but clearly he'd shaved this morning, and his tie was still tight around his muscular neck. And she needed to get a grip—*his neck?* What the hell was wrong with her?

The common room was too casual, intimate. Especially with her inconvenient and really fricking stupid attraction. "Come on into the office."

Penny led him into Heather and Michael Tully's cramped office. She flipped on the bright lights, dispelling the dark, and banishing the intimacy from the common room.

The Tullys didn't spend much time here. They preferred to be out and about at the camp. And they lived in Serenity Cottage on the camp grounds. But the office captured the essence of their commitment to recreating summer camp for adults.

Diego Ramos had been mostly silent, but she could feel his gaze on her.

Once they were inside the office, she headed around the desk so she could put some distance between them. "Have a seat." Sitting behind the desk, safely far away from his too sexy body, appealed to her.

He moved with a liquid assurance, appearing relaxed but still…buttoned up. Every hair in place, his clothes perfect. His pants sharply creased, his shirt only slightly rumpled even though it was ten o'clock at night.

Penny shuddered. She couldn't imagine spending all day cooped up inside. "Feel free to relax a little." The wine simmering through her system loosened her thoughts and she suppressed a giggle. She'd like to relax with him.

Another flush spread through her. Thank goodness, he couldn't read her mind.

An air of containment wrapped around him, as if he hadn't relaxed in a long time. Her memories of him were different. When he was younger, his black hair had been a halo of curls around his face. He'd been loose, especially when he'd been leading them on a hike or showing the campers how to bait a hook. The only time she'd seen him uptight and angry was the last time she spoke to him in the parking lot. And that was twenty years ago.

Get over yourself, Penny. She sure wasn't the same.

He still hadn't relaxed enough to sit, and his presence seriously flustered her. Her gaze zoomed around the room until she settled on the giant bulletin board, an oversized calendar in the center showed the activities for the weekend, and circling the official schedule were pictures of couples.

He directed his attention to the board. He sauntered over to the calendar. "Who are all these people?"

"Ah, the camp is getting a reputation for bringing couples together."

She sighed, thinking about the lovely story of how Heather and Michael Tully had met at the camp, gotten married, separated, and then reunited to make the dream of Camp Firefly Falls for adults come to fruition.

He studied the board. "You mean all these people hooked up?"

Penny flushed. Hooked up? No. Connected in a meaningful way and decided to combine their lives. Romance? Yes.

It was almost as if the Tully's rekindled love affair had started a trend.

That certainly wouldn't happen with her. She didn't have time for romance, even if occasionally she wished she did.

"Found lasting love," she said firmly. She wasn't going to diminish the commitment of the camp couples. Between her stiff shoulders and clenched teeth, her tone was stilted and a little snooty.

His eyebrows bent into a frown, as he shifted his attention from the photos to Penny. "Have we met?"

Penny jolted. She really didn't want to get into the last time they'd shared the same air. A shame and guilt she'd never quite gotten over flushed through her.

His stomach growled.

"Oh, you're hungry." She jumped up from behind the desk. "Let me see what we've got in the kitchen." And she ran out of the office like her butt was on fire.

Her heart thundered in her chest as she yanked open the commercial SubZero fridge searching for something to feed Diego Ramos.

She'd thought of him often but, her memory was more of a caricature, representing her societal awakening rather than an actual person. But now he was here and gorgeous and all grown up and sexy.

And so very real.

She grabbed a bowl of chicken salad from the bottom shelf and shoved the door shut. She'd brought this from home so she knew it wasn't needed for the opening tomorrow.

"Can I help?" His voice feathered over the back of her neck. Unexpectedly close.

She whirled around. "Holy manure." Startled, she lost her grip on the stainless steel bowl.

Oh no!

She grabbed for the bowl at the same time as Diego.

Bam. They clunked heads. But he still managed to catch the heavy metal bowl before it hit the tile floor.

"Ow." Penny rubbed her head where they'd connected. "Sorry about that."

Diego Ramos's eye twitched but besides that small flinch his face was impassive. "You okay?"

"Of course." She laughed, a little embarrassed chuckle. She was always okay. There wasn't any other way to be. "You need ice?"

"No, thank you."

Penny bustled around the kitchen opening and closing cabinet doors searching for plates. Where the hell was Meg? "Have a seat and I'll fix you a plate."

"It's not necessary."

Penny dug through the produce drawers and found some romaine lettuce. She arranged the leaves on the simple white plate, then she scooped a generous portion onto the leaves and garnished the salad with a sprig of dill.

"We aim to serve at Camp Firefly Falls." She smiled at him without meeting his gaze.

After plating the food carefully, she settled the offering on the table. "Sorry we only have the kitchen table. He looked like he'd be more at home in a formal dining room, a Georgian table surrounded by claw-footed cherry carved chairs and upholstered with rich gold formal fabric. Kind of like her parent's dining room from her childhood home.

What a seriously bizarre thought. Clearly they'd switched places.

"Thank you. You really didn't have to—"

"I'll just go clear out the common room." She escaped, no other word for it.

DIEGO WASN'T sure what just happened.

He rubbed the tender spot on his head and shrugged. The aroma of the food was getting to him. So he dug in to the best chicken salad he'd ever tasted.

Crunchy sweet apples and celery mixed with tender chicken and a seasoned dressing that held a bit of bite, and sweetness. Diego groaned. Damn, this was good.

"Oh." The chef was back.

Only a long habit of suppressing his reactions kept his face blank. "The chicken salad is excellent."

When was the last time he ate something homemade? Besides a sandwich eaten standing up at his sink?

"Right?" Meg plopped at the table, far more comfortable with him than the missing Penny. "Penny's specialty."

A random, completely inappropriate thought flashed through his brain as he wondered what else Penny was good at.

"Your room is ready."

"Sorry to intrude." Diego stood at the sink and rinsed his plate, then looked around for the dishwasher. Finally, he set the plate in the sink.

"It's all good." Meg grinned. "But tomorrow is a busy day. So we'd all better hit the sack."

He smiled. "Do I need a password for the internet? I've got a little more work to do tonight."

Penny had come into the kitchen, her arms full of dishes and the almost empty wine bottle. "Now? It's almost eleven." She dumped the dishes in the sink and eyed him speculatively.

"Well, I'm taking nearly three days off for this retreat." He tried to answer reasonably but something about her tone set him on edge. It was none of her damn business if he had work to do. "Business won't run itself."

"There's a difference between hard work and running yourself into the ground." Penny propped her fists on her hips. He ran his gaze down her disheveled appearance.

Meg stepped in between them, trying to defuse the sudden tension in the big industrial kitchen.

"C'mon, Farmer Hastings." Meg slung her arm around Penny's shoulders. "Tomorrow is going to be a long day."

"Hastings? Penny…Penelope Hastings?" he blurted out.

The spoiled, wealthy kid who'd haunted his memories?

The chef glanced between the two of them.

"Yes." Penny straightened, her gaze haughty. Even with the ratty jeans, hair tumbling around her face, and no makeup, this chick could seem like a princess talking to a peasant.

Suddenly he realized why she looked familiar. It was Penelope Hastings. "No wonder you don't know anything about hard work."

Shit. That hadn't come out right.

She stared at him for another second. He swore the air shimmered with how he'd hurt her. Again.

Fuck.

Which seemed crazy. She'd probably never done a day's hard work in her life.

"On that note…" Penny ducked her head and bounded up the stairs.

Meg raised her eyebrows. "Your room is up the stairs, second floor, first door on the right." Her easy demeanor gone, she pressed her lips together like she was holding in harsh words.

But Diego's gaze returned to the retreat of Penelope Hastings. His nemesis and his inspiration and motivation all in one. He'd long ago given up the urge to apologize to her. Assumed he had been a small blip on her summer of '97 camp experience. After all, they'd been kids.

Diego shook off the regret. He had work to do. They couldn't all be wealthy heiresses playing at being a farmer.

"Password?" he gutted out.

Meg rattled it off.

Diego grabbed his leather suitcase from the office and headed up the stairs.

He needed to put in another hour or two of work. But even as he tried to concentrate, his mind wouldn't let go of the memories.

Penelope Hastings. Here at his retreat. Twenty years later, they were both back Camp Firefly Falls.

What were the odds?

$$\approx \quad 3 \quad \ll$$

Penny had slept horribly. Not a surprise.

Even so, she was up at five. Contrary to Diego Ramos's snarky comment, she knew what hard work was.

No sense in showering just yet. Her work would be tough and dirty today. She'd need to be presentable for the opening evening reception but she had twelve plus hours before she had to make an appearance.

Penny wove her hair into two no-nonsense braids, threw some water, then sunscreen on her face, and donned a sports bra, jeans, and her pretty "Nevertheless she persisted" cotton tank top. She tugged on her boots. Then, given the slight chill in the air, she threw a flannel over her tank top.

In the kitchen, she grabbed one of Meg's cinnamon rolls and closed her eyes. "Heaven." As much as she wanted to savor the buttery goodness, she had work to do.

She slugged down a cup of coffee to jump-start her foggy brain.

"Morning." Meg's greeting startled her.

"Notice there wasn't a *good* in there," Penny said wryly. The wine from last night was definitely the impetus for her fuzzy head this morning.

Meg laughed. "I slept great. What was up with you and our camper?"

"Remember that story I told you from my first year at camp? My whiny ass and a grumpy counselor?"

"Yep." Meg took ingredients from the pantry, laying them out on the white marble counters.

"He's the guy."

"Wait, the counselor who yelled at you?" Meg's eyes widened. "Um, wow?"

She wouldn't admit that she'd been keeping track of him since she'd seen the article about Diego Ramos in *FAST* magazine a few years ago. She finished her cinnamon roll, heaven in a pastry, and nodded. "Well, better get started."

Her assistant, Brad, would be here in the next fifteen minutes or so. He was driving up from the farm to help her set up the garden beds for the camp. Her truck bed was filled with 2 x 8 boards, a box of tools, and braces to assemble the beds. Ideally this would have been done ahead of time but during the summer she really couldn't spare the extra time away from the farm, so she'd decided to pack everything into the three-day weekend. As a bonus, she got to spend some time with Meg last night.

The day ahead loomed with hard work and manual labor. She was no gentlewoman farmer, no matter what Diego Ramos thought.

She poured a cup of coffee into a white ceramic mug with "Camp Firefly Falls…back to what really matters" logo and headed outside. She lifted her face to the rising sun.

The chill in the air would burn off later but for right now she needed the flannel overshirt. Her small headache was a combo of a bit too much wine and last night's restless sleep.

Penny's edginess was due strictly to Mr. Gorgeous and Grumpy.

Her dreams had been filled with Diego Ramos. Luscious, sex-filled fantasies that she had no business dreaming since he'd been kind of a dick to her.

So perhaps it had been a little too long since she'd had sex. But after her last boyfriend "encouraged" her to give up the "stupid playing at farming and move back to Boston," she'd sworn off men for a while.

Clearly it might be time to revisit the No Men rule if she was reduced to fantasizing about a jerk rather than say…Luke Evans.

Penny lugged her tools from the trunk of her car, taking a moment to admire the Porsche. Must have been a challenge to get up some of the hills to camp.

She might drive around in an old pickup most of the time but her father had been a connoisseur of fast cars, and some of that had rubbed off on her.

The chug of her farm truck's engine hit her ears. Penny waved down Brad. "Morning. Thanks for getting up here early."

"No problem, Penny." Brad was bright-eyed and eager, like a puppy. He ran through what he'd already done this morning and she was thankful she'd found him.

Penny unhooked the gate on the back of the pickup. "Go grab a cup of coffee and one of Meg's cinnamon rolls. I'll start unloading."

She'd been able to grab a cart to make the transfer of raw materials for the raised beds a little easier.

Penny pulled the cart, which looked like it had been swiped straight from Home Depot, to the back of the truck. Then she started taking the 2 x 8 boards from the truck bed and setting them on the metal cart. She dropped one by accident and it echoed with a loud clang.

Oops.

Once it was sufficiently loaded, Penny pushed the cart through the grass and to the plot of open land—to the right and the rear of Pinecone Lodge—that the Tullys had agreed to turn into a fun camp experience for their corporate retreaters. And then the camp would reap the benefits of a producing kitchen garden

The cart rumbled over the uneven ground, the heavy lumber bouncing and banging on the in the early morning air. Good thing the corporate people weren't here yet. Penny had managed to eke out three open days in her schedule, today thru Sunday. Yesterday she'd worked a full day at the farm before coming out here.

A giant pyramid of rich loamy soil had been dumped as close to the lodge as possible. The only major obstacle was that she would have to move the fertile soil in small batches. The dump truck that delivered the dirt couldn't get through the trees to the side of the camp where she was going to set up the beds, and the dirt needed to be out of view of the cabins and front of the lodge.

But a water source for irrigation was far more important than dumping the dirt close to the garden. It just meant more physical labor for Penny and her assistant.

Her heart pumped as she finished unloading the wood for the beds.

She lay out the lumber in rows, setting up the lines for the narrow raised beds based on the already installed irrigation system. By the time she'd unloaded all the lumber and supplies, her arms were already complaining. She was going to be completely wrung out before the day was done.

Sweat coated her forehead. She swiped her forearm across her face but the giant glove—meant for Brad's hand—fell off.

She would get started on constructing the frames while Brad got a cup of coffee. Between the two of them they could knock this out in a few hours.

Then she needed Brad to get back to the farm.

The whole point of this experiment was to convince small businesses and corporate clients to install food gardens in their office complexes.

Penny blew a stray strand of hair out of her eyes.

She marked the wood through the holes in the L brackets, then held the pencil between her lips while she checked to make sure the brackets were level. She retrieved her cordless drill and began setting the brackets to connect the first bed. The whirring as the screws penetrated the Northern White Cedar wood soothed her.

For this kind of bed, the construction measurements didn't have to be completely accurate but she tried to be precise in everything she did.

The screen door that led from the kitchen slammed. Penny waved haphazardly at Brad without looking up. She took the pencil out of her mouth and yelled, "'Bout ready!" as she turned.

"What the hell are you doing?" Angry Diego was back. His hair was matted on one side, and dark stubble shadowed his jaw. He hadn't raised his voice a decibel. If anything, the words were more of a hiss.

Penny blinked. What the hell was she doing? Rhetorical or literal?

She went with literal. "Building raised beds."

Beds. Bed. He was clearly fresh out of bed, looking rumpled and sexy and hot.

He wore a white tank undershirt and some hastily thrown-on basketball shorts. His caramel skin gleamed in the soft misty air.

"At—" he glanced at his bare wrist "—really early in the morning? You couldn't wait until the sun was fully up?"

Hot or not, he was starting to piss her off. But Penny had been the object of scorn and ridicule before over something a hell of a lot more personal than a construction project. "Nope."

He rubbed his palm through his short hair. His biceps flexed. Her mouth watered. Literally. And that was unacceptable.

Penny turned and bent to pick up the drill again. His sharp annoyed inhale made her realize she might have miscalculated. He was, after all, a paying customer. "There's coffee in the kitchen," she offered.

Then she started up the drill so that he couldn't talk to her and began connecting the wood boards.

A minute later someone tapped her on the shoulder. She stopped the drill and whirled around. "Look—"

Brad stood there. "Penny." His face was dead white.

"What's wrong?"

He looked like he was going to fall over.

"It's Greg." Brad's boyfriend was still a student at UMass Amherst. "I just got a phone call. He was in an accident."

Penny grabbed his ice cold hands. "Is he going to be okay?"

"I don't—"

"Where's he at?"

He rattled off the hospital name. "I need—"

"To go to the hospital." Penny's day just got a whole lot more complicated. "I don't want you driving."

"Yeah." Tears glimmered in his eyes.

"Give me a sec to put away the tools and let Meg know I'll be back."

Looks like Diego was going to get his wish for quiet after all.

DIEGO DECIDED to get some work done since he was up.

But concentrating was difficult. Penelope Hastings. The girl who had haunted him was all grown up. Until he'd realized who she was, he'd been attracted. *Very* attracted.

He shaved and then showered, thinking about her.

The little spoiled girl had turned into a gorgeous sexy woman. Annoyance churned in his stomach at whatever wild hair she'd gotten to start a construction project so early in the morning. No concept of time or respect for the fact that it was damn early.

He frowned. Damn early.

He'd wanted to run his tongue along her skin and taste

those intriguing freckles. Trail his fingers along her neck and dig into her thick lustrous hair to hold her head for his kiss.

Annoyed with his thoughts and his completely inappropriate urges, he rubbed the towel over his damp body, his thoughts returning without consent to the shadow between her breasts.

And shit. He had an erection.

Down, boy.

His brain flip-flopped between the spoiled little girl and the sexy-as-fuck woman.

Guilt and lust tangled up together, leaving him aroused and frustrated, and wasn't that a weird combo? He threw his towel on the bed in disgust.

Silence.

Was she done? He stared out the window, careful to move the curtain slightly. But no one was there. The wood lay abandoned in the dewed grass, a ray of morning sunlight slanted through the trees revealing the empty area.

She'd stopped work already?

Diego shook his head. He needed to stop thinking about Penelope Hastings and get back to what was important. Business.

He dressed in khakis and a polo. His friend, Jason Hollingsworth the Fourth, had told him from the beginning *Dress like you belong in the boardroom.*

He thanked the random vagaries of fate that he'd had the balls to follow the escapees from Harvard's Young Entrepreneurs workshop into the diner that day all those years ago. Except he would have never been trying to sneak in to that exclusive seminar if he hadn't taken Penelope

Hastings's advice to heart. And…he was thinking about her again.

While he called Zinnia, Diego stared out the window, taking in the rustic surroundings. Meg had given him a corner room. While he could see where Penny had begun her project on the side, out the other window, in the distance the sunlight glistened on Lake Waawaatesi. A single row of cabins arched from one end of camp to the other along the shore, mostly concealed by the woods. He didn't have anything in his closet appropriate for a weekend at camp. He'd been thinking the facilities would be more retreat-ish than primitive.

"Well played," he said after Zinnia answered the phone.

"Ah, you're there?"

"Yes," he said patiently.

"I didn't want you to be late."

He loved his cousin, so he let it go. "I need you to pick up some more casual clothes for me."

"From your apartment?"

"From the store. Get me cargo shorts, bring a few company T-shirts, board shorts swimsuit, and a pair of Sperry's."

He was a fair boss. He tried to inspire loyalty while still maintaining authority. Of course, he'd grown up with Zin. So maybe she had less fear of him than his regular employees.

"Yes, boss." The contrition in her voice was easy to hear but then she perked up. "Is it like you remembered?"

Penelope's features popped into his brain. "Not at all."

"Better?" She was so hopeful, so enthusiastic. She'd

never gotten to go to summer camp. By the time she was old enough, Camp Firefly Falls had closed.

"Sure."

Zinnia let out a sigh. "See you later, *mi hermano*."

"And, Zin?"

"Yeah?" She was back to her perky self.

"You owe me."

Diego settled at the desk and opened his laptop. A few hours later, the rumble of a gorgeous engine caught his attention. The '69 Charger was back. He stopped working and waited.

He wasn't sure why but the fact that she owned a Charger seemed wrong. Which was ridiculous. But dammit, that was *his* car. What was she doing driving one?

He admitted to being a voyeur when instead of getting back to work, he watched Penelope Hastings trudge toward the job she'd started earlier. His previous frustration had shifted. She couldn't be that much of a slacker if she'd been up at five a.m.

She opened the giant toolbox. She studied the boards on the ground then visibly straightened her shoulders and got down to work.

He couldn't say why but her posture struck a chord of shame in him.

Why was she so upset?

4

Penny had gotten half the boxes screwed together.

She took a break and drank from her ecologically-friendly, reusable water bottle.

Worry for Brad's boyfriend thrummed beneath the surface, but her mind kept returning to Diego Ramos. The man was hot, hot, hot.

The sexy stubble that darkened his jaw, his defined biceps, flat stomach where his thin T-shirt clung to the rippled abs, and the silky shorts that did nothing to hide his impressive bulge.

Daydreaming about things that were never going to happen was counterproductive, and she needed to pick up the pace on these boxes. The Tullys would be back soon for camp registration at two.

She looked up at the sky and noted she didn't have much time.

She sighed.

"What's wrong?"

She jumped about a foot in the air and whirled around. "You sure are quiet."

Diego stood closer than she expected, dressed like he was on his way to the country club for a round of golf. His cheeks were smooth and she couldn't help but remember the scruff that framed his lips earlier this morning. Without her permission, her gaze tracked to his mouth.

His unsmiling mouth.

Penny jerked her attention back to his eyes. In the meantime, his gaze heated and dropped to her lips. Suddenly the air around them turned soupy, thick with sexual tension and the rising humidity.

"How come you stopped earlier?"

"My assistant's boyfriend was in an accident. I had to get him to the hospital."

She swiped at her brow again. Diego stepped closer, lifted his hand to her cheek.

Penny stepped back. "What are you doing?" But her voice was shaky.

"You had some dirt. On your face."

She took another step back, skimmed her gaze down his body. He was all neat and proper. "You don't want to mess up your clothes."

"I'll survive." Diego smiled faintly.

The air was supercharged. A subtle sexual tension hovered in the air; she was hyper-aware of him.

"So what are the raised beds for?"

He had no idea? But he was the boss and the Tullys had confirmed the addition with their company liaison.

"Part of this weekend retreat's mission is to introduce sustainable gardening into corporate culture."

She waited for his derision. He certainly hadn't been very open since they'd reconnected.

He seemed to be waiting expectantly for more information. Except Penny had to get back to work. "Don't take this the wrong way…but in order to get this done before the welcome reception, I need to work while I talk."

"Multi-tasking." He grinned, his teeth white in his swarthy face and his eyes, the color of a dark espresso, crinkled. "I'm familiar with it."

The power of that smile nearly dropped her to her knees. She wanted to bask in that glow, but she had raised beds to build.

"Why do corporations need gardens?"

He sounded intrigued rather than disdainful, and she figured educating the CEO couldn't hurt. "Multiple studies show that being in nature for even a short time each day increases productivity, creates a more focused mind, relieves stress, relieves inflammation—which means less employee sick days."

Penny struggled to set the board in place. Diego stepped closer and steadied it for her. "You'll get dirty," she protested.

"I can also get clean." He braced the board so she could drill in the screws. As the day had warmed up, she'd used a wide headband to keep the escaping strands of hair off her face.

She smiled. His appearance didn't suggest that he'd gotten dirty since he was a kid. She got lost in the deep mystery of his gaze.

"Corporate gardens?"

"Oh, um, yeah." She ducked her head and focused on

screwing together the boards. "Working in the soil and with nature provides a benefit to the employees. The food harvested can either be used by the company or donated to a local food pantry."

"What's in it for you?"

She wanted to bristle but she kept her tone calm, even. "I charge a consulting fee to design and set up the gardens."

"Most companies don't need the food. They either have a food service in place or the employees are on their own." His point was a good one.

She and Diego had settled into an easy rhythm. He anticipated her moves before she even finished, and she continued explaining her idea.

"Then they take the charitable contribution and create goodwill in their local community. It's a win-win."

And if one less kid went hungry, everybody won.

"Let's get these beds lined up." She'd gotten so used to him anticipating that she forgot he wasn't just there to work for her.

On three they lifted the first wood frame and moved it into place.

Together they worked easily to lay out the six beds into two even rows of three. The silence was effortless, reflective, until it wasn't.

Step one: done.

Penny avoided looking at him, choosing instead to study the area she'd already staked out. She still had to get the dirt distributed in the six beds.

"How in the world did *you* ever get into farming?"

There was the disdain she'd been expecting earlier. The disappointment that flooded her wasn't a surprise. The bigger surprise was that he'd taken so long to be disparaging.

That was a discussion that they could have, oh…never.

"Degree in Ag from UMass Amherst." She picked up the tools and loaded them into the toolbox. Next up was distributing the soil into the beds. The tools could go back in her truck.

"Not very Middlesex County of you," he mocked.

Yeah, well, she'd left the Brahmin crowd behind. Or they'd left her behind, as it were.

"Hard to believe you muck around in the dirt. The kid I remember was always pristine. Even after a week of camp your shoes were still bleach white."

He remembered her shoes?

"I like being dirty," she said defensively, then the alternative meaning of her words sank in. An embarrassed flush began in her stomach and spread outward.

"In the right circumstances, *dirty* can be really good." His voice pitched low, deepening.

Oh my *Gawd*. Desperate to shift the conversation, she said the first thing that popped into her head. "How's that Porsche?"

"Fantastic." But he was studying her, like he wanted to dissect her, pin her down, and discover all her secrets.

A commotion from the front of Pinecone Lodge interrupted whatever he'd been about to ask.

"Hey! I brought your clothes." A gorgeous young, maybe twenty-two, Latina girl tossed a bag at him. She had waves of long curls with a deep purple streak along her left temple, capri jeans, and a tight T-shirt spread across her generous breasts. Together they made a stunning couple, all dark hair, dark skin and dark eyes, like the Boston equivalent of Penelope Cruz and Javier Bardem.

The woman skidded to a stop in front of them. Blinked at the dirt that smudged his khakis and the sweat dampening his shirt. "Just in time." She laughed as she said it but she couldn't seem to take her eyes off Diego.

And that was Penny's cue to get back to work.

"I checked us in." The girl looked at Diego expectantly.

He nodded curtly.

"Sorry about the mix-up on your calendar."

Diego snorted. "Mix-up? Is that what we're calling it?" Even sweaty and slightly dirty, he was hot. And seeing him with the young cutie, Penny had enough. She still had hours of work ahead of her.

Well, this had been fun. Or not. But she couldn't let him leave without thanks. "Thanks for your help."

The girl's jaw dropped. "Wait. You helped?"

"Zinnia." He glared.

"Sorry," she muttered, her gaze skimming over the morning's work.

"No rest for me." Penny dismissed him. "Have fun at camp."

She had hours to go before her first official camp duties.

Diego raised his eyebrows. "You need any more help?"

"I've got it." And she turned away from the sexy CEO and his gorgeous girlfriend.

5

Diego did not want to be here.

Cocktail parties were his least favorite part of being the CEO of his company. He had to attend them. He'd copped to that fact a long time ago but he still didn't like them.

He sipped his beer from the bottle, because yeah, he might be in the corporate suite now but he'd grown up in a garage surrounded by no-nonsense mechanics who saw no need to dirty a glass when the bottle worked just fine.

Around him, his employees mingled with the employees of London Automotive. He smiled tightly at Jeffrey London, the CEO of the business he was looking to merge with.

"This was a good idea." Jeffrey London sipped on some fancy concoction with a sprig of greenery. "Quaint, provincial, and neutral for both companies."

They were as opposite as hot and cold. Jeffrey came from a long line of upper crust Bostonians who had been in the states since the Mayflower, while Diego was second generation Puerto Rican from Dorchester. His parents hadn't fared well here—that was putting it nicely— and Tío Raul had been an Army mechanic before he opened his garage.

On paper, their companies meshed extremely well. But in person, Diego had a hard time sustaining conversation that didn't pertain to business with London.

"I can't take credit." Because Diego believed in transparency and giving recognition where it was due. "My assistant, Zinnia, suggested a corporate retreat. She found the venue and designed the program with the owners." They'd rented out the entire camp for their private function.

The welcome cocktail party was in the old boathouse, which the owners had decorated with little white twinkling lights. A rustic bar set up in the corner served drinks, and round tables with white tablecloths and what looked like twigs and pinecones from the woods were piled in the center of the tables. The nature stuff was lumped artistically around flickering candles, he'd give them that.

He smiled politely at London and wondered how long he needed to stay at the party. He couldn't wait to get back to his cabin and crash.

Penny Hastings slipped through the large doors of the boathouse. In a long flowy dress in a sage green, her auburn hair loose, cascading over her shoulders and curling delicately over her breasts, she glowed.

Delicate, vulnerable, ethereal.

She looked like a wood nymph or fairy. All she needed was flowers twined in her hair and she'd blend in with the woods as if she belonged there.

And Jesus, what was wrong with him? Wood nymph? Fairy?

He'd helped her this morning, her ethic more like a sturdy workhorse than a soft fictional creature. Diego shook off the fanciful thoughts and observed her. He seemed to be the only one at the party who noticed her hesitation at the entrance.

"Well, who is that?" London's frosty demeanor perked up. "One of yours?"

"No."

Before Diego could say more, London said, "Perhaps I'll go introduce myself."

London's wife was not in attendance. She'd gone to Europe for the summer, which Diego knew because the man had mentioned it at least twice in conversation.

"That's Penny," Diego drawled. "She's visiting staff for the camp."

He hoped that since she was "the help" that might put London off. But if anything his attitude brightened even further.

"An introduction, please."

He couldn't approach her on his own? Diego gritted his teeth. "Sure."

Michael Tully paused next to Penny and spoke to her for a few minutes. She nodded and he headed out of the boathouse. He'd mentioned earlier that Heather, their regular camp director and Michael's wife, had the stomach flu.

After Michael left, Penny drifted around the room, pausing to speak with each group of people. Her smile open and relaxed, her face animated as she spoke with her hands. She charmed everyone she met. But her energy seemed to be waning as she made her way toward the bar, and Diego.

Earlier when they parted, he'd had the feeling she was annoyed with him. For which he had no idea why. After all, he'd helped her set up her damn boxes.

But he flagged her down anyway. If possible he'd try to warn her about London. Since he was Boston society, he was sort of surprised that Jeffrey London and Penny didn't know each other.

Finally Diego was able to catch her attention. "Penny, this is Jeffrey London, CEO of London Automotive."

"Nice to meet you." She smiled but the weariness beneath her curling lips seemed obvious to Diego.

Then he realized she'd been going strong since five a.m. and it was closing in on nine. The sun had begun to set. The last time he'd seen her, when he'd moved his duffel from the lodge to his private cabin, she'd been sweaty and dusted in dirt from moving wheelbarrows full of soil from the giant pile to the beds.

"Pleasure is all mine." Jeffrey lifted her hand to his lips, kissing her skin.

Really? Did that actually work?

And he wondered how Jeffrey London would feel if he knew that an hour ago Penny had been covered in fertilized loamy soil.

Penny removed her hand from London's. Her expression didn't change, but Diego sensed her discomfort. He leaned closer, "Can I get you a drink?"

"Just a club soda." Her husky voice triggered a rush of arousal that took him unawares. "Thank you."

"London?"

"Another of these." Jeffrey London tossed back the rest of his cocktail and handed Diego the glass.

"So, Penny." London literally turned his back on Diego to push them into a small bubble. "What is it you will be doing?"

Diego waited for a drink at the bar. The rest of the camp would be family-style meals and self-service bars but for the first night Zinnia had set up a more formal cocktail party. After the groups checked in, they had gotten tours of the camp grounds and activities available. Zin had presided over a quick ice-breaker activity that Diego had avoided. He hadn't had a chance to check in with her to see how it went. Prior to this weekend, the employees from the two companies—with the exception of Diego, London, and their attorneys—hadn't interacted.

When he got back to the pair, Penny was lecturing animatedly about her corporate garden program.

Jeffrey London might want in her pants, but he clearly had no interest in her project. His eyes were glazed, from a combo of boredom and consuming three martinis in less than an hour.

"Thank you, Ramos."

Diego inclined his head. "Not a problem."

Penny smiled gratefully. "Thanks."

"So Farmer Hastings was pitching her employee garden idea?"

At first when she'd explained, he hadn't been convinced, but the more she talked about the project her enthusiasm was contagious. And after just a day in the woods, and helping her, working with his hands, he was calmer, more relaxed, and feeling a sense of peace. While he needed to see more financial data and consider the startup costs, the idea was growing on him.

"Hastings?" Jeffrey London sneered. "Penelope Hastings?"

Penny lifted her chin, the vulnerable animated woman gone. "Yes."

London snorted. "See you tomorrow, Ramos." He disappeared into the crowd.

"Well, I'd best mingle some more." Penny's smile was forced, stiff, and she wouldn't meet his eyes.

Diego frowned as she stalked away. What was that about?

❦

PENNY CREPT out of the boathouse and headed for the dock.

God, she ached.

She sat on the dock, removed her strappy sandals, dipped her toes in the cool water, and lay back. The dark blue evening sky sparkled with stars. Peace settled over her as she relaxed against the warm wood. Sounds filtered in, a dreamy ballad playing in the boathouse, crickets chirping, the woods rustling with nocturnal creatures. Fireflies lit the campground, and the water from Lake Waawaatesi lapped gently against the pilings.

She let exhaustion wash over her. Once she'd stopped hauling the dirt, her arm muscles had stiffened almost immediately. Jeez, she was tired.

Penny's jaw cracked as she yawned. Her eyes drifted closed as she listened to the music of nature.

She'd lived through plenty of cocktail parties when she'd been a kid. Learned the art of small talk and how to identify the overserved in the room with just a glance. Attending a formal party never failed to remind her of her former life, the good and the bad all rolled in one.

She used to love getting dressed up. Her mother's maid would curl her hair, and if it was a particularly special occasion, sometimes Penny would get to put a flower in her hair and be allowed to wear a little lip gloss.

But attending parties now reminded her of what happened after her parents had skipped the country and the news they'd swindled hundreds of thousands of dollars from their customers became common knowledge. The public censure on her, as if she'd had something to do with their crimes, had been intense. Jeffrey London certainly brought all that back. Eleven years and she was still being judged for her parents' crimes.

Looking on the bright side, she would not be where she was today if that girl, who liked dressing up and attending parties, had grown up the way her life had originally been destined.

And she liked who she was, what she did.

She'd had enough money from her grandmother to purchase a working farm after college. She tended her organic farmland and hired kids from the local Ag programs to learn the business and help with labor. With her minor in accounting, she did her own books and was completely self-sufficient.

She loved her life, barring the fact that she was sometimes lonely. Late at night after her employees were gone and the chores were done for the day, it would be nice to share a meal with a lover. Share the mundane details of her day with someone. But if that's all she had to complain about, she was incredibly lucky.

The musical sounds of the night lulled her into a semi-conscious state. She drifted on the summer night's breeze, content to let everything flow around her.

"Penny?" Diego's husky voice rumbled from the shore.

Dress shoes, loafers maybe, scuffed against the dock. Penny lay there knowing she'd have to get up in a second to resume her role as an ambassador for corporate gardens and the camp.

But for one more lovely moment, she just was.

"Penny." An urgency that hadn't been evident threaded Diego's voice. He was running now. "Are you—is everything—"

She sat up abruptly and he skidded to a stop. "I was just admiring the stars." She tilted her head back and stared at the sky. Had that been panic in his voice?

"Jesus." He dropped down next to her. He gulped the rest of his beer and put the bottle on the dock with a thud.

Since she couldn't very well comment on his unexpected concern, she searched for a safe topic. The weather. The outdoors. Innocuous subjects. "Gorgeous night."

"Yeah." Diego cleared his throat. "I don't spend much time outside."

"That's a shame."

He shrugged, and his biceps brushed her shoulder. The light contact should have been nothing, a mere whisper against her bare skin, but her nerve endings suddenly sizzled with awareness.

Diego Ramos was close. His body radiated a subtle heat, warming her left side. A shiver shimmied over her spine.

"Cold?" The question was hushed in the quiet night air.

Lights from the cabins twinkled along the paths, but out here on the dock, dark wrapped around them, protecting their privacy.

Sexual awareness shimmered between them, thick in the humid air.

"I'm fine." But a little tremor in her voice gave her away.

"What was that all about?"

She didn't pretend not to understand. "You sure are direct."

"I live by a few credos, one of which is you never know unless you ask."

She raised her eyebrows, her lips curled in a smirk. "That's certainly true."

But she didn't answer.

The urge to rest her head on his shoulder, to lean against him even for a moment, was so strong. She yearned for that physical closeness.

"How was your day?" she asked, desperately wanting him to focus on something other than the way Jeffrey London had snubbed her.

ⓈⒶⒹ

DIEGO WAS SILENT FOR A MOMENT. How was his day? "Fine." Not exactly the truth but nothing that he could pinpoint was wrong. And yet dissatisfaction thrummed below the surface of his emotions. He couldn't seem to shake this restlessness that plagued him more and more.

He'd rather think about Penny and their illicit attraction

than his strange unsettled feelings about today's merger meeting. But that topic should be a no-go too.

He couldn't reconcile her hard work with his memories of the spoiled little girl, but she wasn't a little girl any longer. She was a lush, sexy, earthy woman who pushed all his buttons, even some he didn't realize he had.

"Well, I'd best get to bed," Penny said.

His breath caught. Images of them in bed twined together, his dark flesh an erotic contrast to her fairer skin. His hand against her breast, her fingers clutching his shoulders as he tasted her. The visual images brought his libido to stunning immediate life.

"I'll walk you to your cabin." Diego jumped to his feet, pleasantly sore from his work today, and tried to banish those erotic visions from his brain. *No sex with the help.* And okay, shit he sounded like Jeffrey London right there.

No sex. Period. This weekend was to finalize the deal that would move him from a well-off millionaire into the upper echelons of billionaire CEO status.

After many years—sweat, heartbreak, and learning curves—he was within reach of the goal he'd been striving for since her words struck him during their altercation in the parking lot all those summers ago.

Penny hesitated another second. He held out his hand. Tentatively she placed her palm in his and he tugged her to her feet. Except she'd already started to stand, and the combined efforts propelled her right into him.

"Oh." She lost her balance, falling against him, her breasts rubbing his chest. Her soft exhale puffed against his lips and they tingled.

He still held her balled fingers. He tugged her even

tighter against his body and curled his other arm around her waist so they were pressed together from knee to collarbone. He stared into her shadowed green eyes, barely able to see her features. The new moon offered little visibility.

Her eyes fluttered shut. Giving him permission or shutting him out? He bent his head and paused a hairsbreadth from her mouth. "I'm going to kiss you." Business 101, use declarative sentences to state your intentions rather than as a question.

"Mm'kay."

He brushed his lips against hers, butterfly soft. He didn't want to scare her. She was already skittish, as if she would bolt if he let go.

What the hell was he doing, kissing Penelope Hastings?

Probably the worst idea he'd ever had and yet… He sipped at her mouth, learning the texture. Her arms were toned and her hands callused and strong, and her lips were soft, sweet.

She melted against him, and her free arm circled his shoulders and held on as if he was the only thing keeping her from liquefying into a puddle on the ground. Her soft moan of acquiescence spurred him on.

The scent of lilacs rose in the heated air. She scraped her fingernails along his scalp and his dick hardened in a rush. Ever since that moment in the kitchen last night, he'd been thinking about kissing her. More than kissing her.

She sighed and opened for him. Her surrender easy, simple. Between one breath and the next she traced his mouth with the tip of her tongue, dipping inside in an uncomplicated stroke. But as she tried to retreat, he sucked her tongue inside his mouth. And the gentle, tender kiss turned fiercely passionate. Lust swamped him.

Diego slanted his head and dove into the kiss.

She moaned louder as the kiss became a battle. He skimmed his fingers along her back and pressed her ass so that she rocked into his erection.

Twined together, he held tight to her fist, having the irrational thought that if he let go of her hand, she'd flit away.

A shout from the boathouse interrupted their escalating embrace.

They broke apart. Diego's chest heaved as he strained for breath.

Her eyes were wide, shocked, as they stood there, stopped on the precipice of a monumental mistake.

The commotion in the boathouse continued.

"Better see what's wrong." He brushed her loose hair away from her face.

"Yeah."

They headed toward the noise.

When they entered the boathouse, Zinnia was sitting on the makeshift dance floor, tears tracking down her face. She didn't typically drink but he'd noticed earlier she'd been over-imbibing.

"What happened, Zin?"

"Twisted my ankle, knocked over some chairs, hit my head." Her lower lip stuck out like it had when she'd been two. "Generally made an ass of myself."

"All in a day's work." He brushed his thumbs over her tears.

She snorted. But then her eyes filled again. "Hurts," she whispered.

"I can take a look if you'd like," Penny offered. "I have basic first aid training."

"Does the camp have a doctor?"

"All the employees are certified in first aid and obviously CPR but for anything more serious, we rely on the hospital." Penny gestured to a chair. "Let's get her up on the chair so I can take a look."

Diego lifted Zinnia onto the chair and tried to disperse the crowd around her. "She'll be okay. Go ahead and enjoy the party."

But the accident busted the party atmosphere and people paraded by, giving Zin either sympathetic looks or accusing stares, until soon the giant room was empty except for the servers and bartenders.

Penny asked Zin questions, pressing on various spots. But when Penny tried to rotate the injured ankle, Zin cried out. Purple already mottled her skin, and the muscles and tendons around the joint had puffed to twice their normal size.

Someone had grabbed the first aid kit off the wall. Penny wrapped Zin's ankle tightly in a bandage. Then she pulled on the exam gloves and pressed against Zinnia's skull. "Ow."

Penny swabbed the cut and bump with an alcohol wipe, then tossed the gloves and supplies in the garbage.

Diego squatted beside Zin and held her hand. "Everything will be fine."

"I ruined your party." Tears dripped off her chin, likely exacerbated by the cocktails she'd been chugging.

"*Mija*, you planned the party. And you did a great job. Everyone had a blast."

Penny cocked her head at Diego.

He patted Zin's knee gently and stepped away from her.

"She needs to be looked at by a doctor." Penny propped her hands on her hips. "I don't think she has a concussion but I'm pretty sure her ankle is broken. If it isn't broken it's a bad sprain."

Diego pulled out his cell but Penny shook her head. "Won't work out here."

No cell. He'd forgotten.

He rubbed his hand over his head. Zinnia had begun to cry softly again. "Can we call an ambulance at the lodge?"

"It will be faster if we just take her." Penny let her shoulders slump for a second. "Let me wash up and then I'll bring my car down to the boathouse."

"I can take her."

But Penny was shaking her head. "Can't let you do that. You've been drinking and your employee was injured on camp grounds. The Tullys, and their insurance company, would ream me if I let you drive. I'll take her."

"Then I'm going with you."

$\mathscr{H}$ 6 $\mathscr{H}$

Penny was having the most delicious dream.

She was warm and protected and turned on.

She snuggled closer to that warmth and sighed. A slight thump beat beneath her cheek, the sound steady and comforting.

The dream flowed in a series of disjointed pictures, but Diego Ramos featured prominently. Kissing her. Sexing her up. Chatting about their days. Working in the garden. Driving fast in his Porsche. His tenderness, concern, total hotness created a longing she couldn't contain. His devotion to his assistant—and *cousin*, she had finally discovered—was extremely attractive. He didn't abandon her like—

"Penny." The rumble echoed throughout her. "Wake up, sweetheart."

Sweetheart?

As much as she liked that, she didn't have a sweetheart.

Dream. Must be a dream. She snuggled back into the bliss of sleep. So tired.

"Penny."

She swiped her hand, trying to get the voice to go away. Instead someone heaved her. Disoriented, she peeled her eyes open.

Darkness. She blinked.

"I need your help getting Zinnia into her cabin," the voice to her left said.

What? She shook her head trying to clear her brain. She was in her car, in the passenger seat, which never happened.

"You with me?"

She turned her head, and saw him in the dim light. "Diego?"

"Yeah." He brushed her hair from her face and curled it behind one ear. She shivered at the light touch. "Can you help me get Zinnia inside?"

Penny shook off the last of her sleepiness. She'd crashed hard on the way home from the hospital.

Let's hope she hadn't drooled on his shoulder. And thank God he had no idea what she'd been dreaming about.

"Yes, sure." Penny twisted around in her seat. Getting Zinnia into the back seat had been a challenge but she needed to keep her foot propped up and there wasn't enough room in the front seat of the car for that. "Absolutely. Let's get her to bed."

Bed. And Diego and that dream. Penny's face heated but it was pretty dark out so hopefully Diego hadn't noticed. *Focus, Pen.*

Zinnia was passed out in the back seat, probably from a combo of exhaustion and the pain medicine they had given her.

Penny bolted out of the car.

It took twenty awkward minutes to get Zinnia into her cabin and resting in her bed.

The entire time Zinnia had rambled about a variety of things, touching on her worry that Diego wouldn't participate in the activities tomorrow. Apparently he'd blown off the opening ice breaker.

They were just about to leave when Zinnia grabbed Penny's hand. "Promise me."

Penny blinked. She patted Zinnia on the shoulder. "Sure."

Zinnia's grip was tight on Penny's fingers. She shot a blurred, hazy look at Diego. "Make sure he participates in all the activities, including the partner ones. He needs to set a good example."

Penny didn't know how she was supposed to do that. Especially since she barely knew him. But, "Sure."

Zinnia wouldn't let go of Penny's hand. "Diego. I'm supposed to be your partner. You better still participate."

"Yeah, Zin." She snatched at his hand, missing the first time.

"On your word," Zin demanded. "You won't back out."

He was silent, holding her hand loosely, looking as if he desperately wanted to argue.

"How do we turn this failure into a success?" Her words were slurred and her lids drooped. "See, I'm finally getting it."

Penny started at the words. That's what her father always said. Always. Until in the ultimate failure, he fled the country with her mother, leaving Penny behind to face the consequences of their failures.

She'd begun to think that Diego Ramos hadn't really

remembered the last time they'd spoken when they were kids. Because he'd never given any indication that he recalled the scene in the parking lot.

Penny flushed. Clearly, he hadn't completely forgotten.

"I want this camp, this retreat," Zinnia clarified, "to be a success."

"The merger will go through no matter how the camp goes, Zin."

"Don't care about the stupid merger," Zinnia's words slurred even more. "Care about *you*. Participate. Have fun. Be happy."

Penny wanted to slink outside when the conversation turned personal.

"Sure, Zin." Diego pressed a kiss to her forehead. "I promise. Go to sleep. I'll check on you in the morning."

Diego Ramos clearly doted on his cousin. The expression on his face had been soft, affectionate.

They exited Zinnia's cabin.

He handed her the car keys. The quiet pressed in. They were all alone in the hushed woods. "I'll ride with you back to the lodge."

"Oh, I'm not there now. I moved to an employee cabin."

"Then I'll walk you to your cabin." The camp was quiet. The partiers and staff had gone to bed hours ago.

"I'd forgotten the silence of the woods." He inhaled deeply.

"Yeah. Me too." She loved the simple, reflective peace here.

They stood for a few moments, letting the reverent quiet surround them. She spent plenty of time outdoors. But his comment piqued her curiosity. "Where do you live?"

"Boston," Diego replied. "It's never quiet there."

In tacit agreement, they walked toward her cabin.

She rarely visited the city anymore. Her life was in the western part of the state. Of course, if she got this side business off the ground, she'd have to be in the city more often. But right now, nature was her groove. "Chickens and roosters are a little different from traffic and sirens."

"You actually live on a farm?"

She decided not to take offense. "Yep. Ride a tractor and everything."

"That's slightly slower than my GT," he teased.

Soon they were at her cabin door. "Thank you."

"It's the least I could do." His mouth curved up in a tired smile.

Penny sighed. Damn, she was exhausted. And she was going to have to go get the plants tomorrow. Brad was still at the hospital with his boyfriend—she'd checked in on him while Diego was helping Zinnia in the emergency room.

And apparently she was participating in activities with Diego.

"Well." Awkward silence filled the air. This felt more like the end of a date than a quick walk home. But she hadn't been on a date in…forever. "I've got a really early day."

He snorted. "On a mission to wake camp up early again and then stop?"

As if she'd planned this morning. "A farmer's work is never done." She infused her voice with a lightness she didn't feel.

His face sobered. "By the way, your engine is running a little rough. You might want to get it looked at."

"I know." She rolled her eyes. If he started mansplaining, this convo was done.

Right now, she was pouring all her extra cash into getting this additional project off the ground. She couldn't afford to spend money on a nonessential repair. As long as it ran, she was good to go.

What was she waiting for? Idiot. This wasn't a date. They weren't even really friends. More like slightly combative acquaintances…who kissed on the dock. She turned to open her door. Stopped to read the note attached to the little knocker.

Penny, call me when you get in. No matter the time. I need another favor.

—Michael Tully

Diego curled his fingers around her biceps and turned her around to face him. "Wait." He pressed his other palm against the doorframe and leaned close. Caged between the hard door and his hard body, her heart thudded, picking up in rhythm.

"Thank you for helping me with Zinnia." He bent his head, his mouth hovering over hers. His gaze asking for permission. The sexual tension simmered between them, heavy in the expectant night air as he waited for her answer.

Penny pressed forward up on her toes, their bodies a mere inch apart. Still she paused but it must have been enough encouragement.

He tugged her against his chest until she snugged tight to his muscles.

She melted against him. There was no other word for it. Her body buzzed with anticipation as she waited for his kiss.

LISA HUGHEY

Everything in her softened and readied for his exploration.

Diego pressed his mouth to hers, his soft lips a contrast to his hard body. His beard scruff tickled her jaw. Her eyes drifted closed and other senses took over. Crickets chirped in the background. Hushed air. Muted sighs. His leg pressed between her thighs as he pinned her to the door.

Their clothing rustled when Penny wrapped her arms around his neck and hung on for the ride.

She sailed on a cloud of lust when he pulled her closer. His kisses harder, she nipped at his mouth. Then he took over, the taste of hospital coffee and the mint from the waiting room subtle as he licked into her mouth. At the rough caress of his tongue against hers, her belly fluttered with desire.

In the growing cycle, there was always that one burst of growth as if all the elements combined in a perfect storm of fertile abundance, and plants budded, moving from the seed stage to an actual green living thing. Her body came alive in that same way with his nurturing commands.

He cupped her ass and rocked her sex into his thigh. Penny moaned, the sound loud among the crickets.

He pulled away from their kiss. Instinctively she wanted to grab him back and continue. But Diego had already backed down the steps. "Thanks again."

"You're welcome."

"See you tomorrow, partner."

Why did that sound more like a threat than a promise?

Summer camp crush.

She had one.

She shut the door and leaned against it, reliving that

66

kiss. Apparently Diego Ramos was good at more than business. He excelled at more earthy pursuits too. He sure was good at kissing. A sunny smile broke over her face. Really good at it.

God, she was tired. Penny quickly changed into her pajamas, little booty shorts and a crop T-shirt. She opened the drawer next to the bed and oh em gee, there were condom packets emblazoned with "Camp Firefly Falls: For the Woody in You." And another with the Red Cross symbol and the caption "Orgasm Donor."

Penny wanted to lay those condom packets underneath her pillow like an adult waiting for the booty call fairy to deliver a sex god to her.

Wouldn't that be nice?

Except she wasn't here to have a sex life. If this corporate retreat went well she'd be launching another business with multi-faceted goals of helping people reduce stress, promoting outreach to get people to eat healthier, and supplying food banks with fresh food. Win-win for everyone.

But without her permission, her imagination supplied Diego shirtless and sweaty. So she didn't need the sex fairy to deliver someone. He was already here. And so totally off-limits that she shouldn't even be thinking about him.

But those moments outside her cabin, laden with intensity and fraught with sexual feelings, overwhelmed her. Her nipples beaded and her core pulsed low in her belly as she imagined Diego naked and intense, sliding in and out of her body with the same effortless grace he'd used to help her this morning.

Then she shut down that line of thought. She was sex dreaming about Diego Ramos. The boy who'd changed her outlook on life once. She needed to forget about him. Now she changed her own outlook.

⚜

DIEGO WOKE SLOWLY. Weirdly, he felt like whistling.

Yesterday, working outside, he'd settled into an easy rhythm with Penny. Even though he hit the gym every morning, his biceps and hamstrings were protesting the unusual use this morning.

He stretched, warming up his sore muscles, his body humming and ready to go. His morning wood had a surprising focus. Penny Hastings.

He'd barely kissed her and he had hardened as if she'd stripped naked and climbed on top of him. Diego took his cock in hand and pumped slowly as the image of Penny on top of him, those small breasts bouncing and head thrown back in ecstasy, took shape in his brain.

He wondered what color her nipples were. The pale pink of her lips or a darker red. He pumped again, his hand rough on his cock as he imagined sucking her into his mouth and playing with her body until she moaned like she'd done on the dock last night.

He really didn't have time to be fantasizing about the farmer woman. His goal for the weekend was to finalize the terms of the merger with Jeffrey London and move forward with his long-term business plans.

But numbers and spreadsheets and mergers blurred as his mind wandered back to her tanned skin, and he imagined kissing her freckles one by one, dipping into her mouth, and lower.

His hand moved faster, as some pre-come leaked from the tip.

His meandering thoughts morphed as he pictured her sliding down his body. Her pink tongue coming out to lap that bit of pre-come up, then closing around his cock and swallowing him whole. Diego groaned and pumped faster.

He was deep in the fantasy blow job when someone knocked on his cabin door. Really? It was six in the morning. And he'd been up until around two a.m. so he ignored the knock. But the person knocking persisted.

When he'd gotten back to his cabin late last night, today's camp schedule had been pinned to his door. And he suddenly remembered what was up for this morning.

Partner yoga? Ha-ha. No.

But since whoever was knocking wouldn't go away, Diego trudged to the door in his boxers. Whoever was stupid enough to wake him up this early would get an eyeful.

He yanked the door open. "What?"

"Zin made me come get you." His cousin Raul Jr., also his VP of shipping, stood in the doorway looking like Diego felt. His black hair stood on end, his indulgence last night evident in his bloodshot eyes and scruff on his face.

"What the hell for?"

Raul groaned. "Yoga."

Diego yawned so hard his jaw cracked. He rubbed his bare chest with his hand and wished he was still deep in his fantasy BJ with the delectable farmer. "No."

"She said you promised."

Fuck.

"What the hell do I wear to yoga?" Diego shuffled to the dresser across from the bed.

"I have no idea." Raul dropped onto the end of Diego's bed. "Shorts, I guess."

Diego found some basketball shorts and a T-shirt with the Ramos CAR logo on it. He tugged them on. "I thought it said partner yoga. I don't have a partner."

"Zin said she took care of it." Raul groaned, dropped his head into his hands.

"What's wrong?"

"What do you think? Hangover. Some of those London guys can really put it away."

"What did you think of them overall?"

Ramos Classic Auto Restoration was privately owned, mostly by Diego and his pal Jason Hollingsworth the Fourth who was a silent partner. But his cousin had a stake in the business, so did every other employee. Nothing incentivized people to work harder than knowing that if the company did well, they earned extra money too.

"Honestly?" Raul's gravelly voice made Diego pause.

"*Sí.*"

"I don't know how the companies will mesh."

Diplomacy wasn't in his cousin's wheelhouse. He usually spoke without thinking and Diego reined him in. He counted on Raul to give him the raw truth. So what was this?

"Why are you holding back?"

"You want to merge. You need to work less." Raul looked away guiltily. "I'm not going to fuck that up for you."

His cousin was protecting him? But that was Diego's job. He was the one who started down this path. He was the one who took care of everyone. He was the one building a life that would mean they never had to worry about money again.

That habitual grinding in his stomach took him by surprise. He had been pain free since yesterday.

Diego glanced at his watch. "I don't have time to discuss this now, I've got to go get my partner. But let's talk later." This wasn't a conversation that should be rushed.

"Who's your partner?"

"Penny Hastings."

"The farmer?" Raul cat-called. "Hey, you don't feel like getting out of bed, for her I'll do any kind of yoga she wants."

Possessiveness flooded him. Penny was his. Diego cuffed his cousin on the head. The surge of annoyance took him by surprise. "Get your own damn partner."

Penny and yoga. Maybe this wouldn't suck after all.

Penny slogged back to her cabin, wading through the early morning mist.

Exhaustion dogged her every step. She glanced at the watch on her wrist. If she skipped breakfast, she could catch a few hours' nap before she had to help with the kayak races.

She'd talked to Michael Tully last night.

Heather's flu had gotten worse and he didn't want to leave her. Because this was a smaller camp than usual, he'd asked for her help. Instead of pitching in on food prep and serving, Penny was supposed to report to the assistant camp director, Tegan. Penny was going to help with the kayak races this morning, serve lunch, and then lead a nature hike and engage the teams for Camp Firefly Falls Bingo this afternoon. Instead of giving her spiel in the lunchroom before the meal, she'd combine her speech with the hike.

All that was good but Penny had personnel issues too, and she still needed to take care of her farm.

So she'd gone home, fed the chickens and pigs, mucked out some stalls, and talked to her neighbors about picking up her chores until Brad was back.

All before six thirty in the morning.

She had more tasks before the kayak races, but hopefully she could grab some sleep. Then as soon as the nursery was open, she was going to arrange for the plants to be delivered. Michael had agreed to pick up the extra cost of delivery so that she could stay here and help out with the camp. She could tailor today's talk to the message that she'd been planning for the conference center. Being out in the woods would be more interesting than the indoor arena anyway.

Since this was her first trial run for implementing her program, she could roll with the changes.

A rustling off to her left had her searching the woods. It was still early. She thought there was some sort of event before breakfast but the only exercise she was getting was two hours of shut eye.

However, she'd prefer not to run into anyone. She'd rolled out of bed after two hours' sleep and tugged on jeans, a flannel, and her work boots. Her braided hair was likely a mess after feeding the animals and pitching fresh hay. Not the proper image for someone trying to convince corporate folks to spend bucks on an experimental program. She had good ideas—if she didn't say so herself—but no practical experience besides her senior thesis project eight years ago.

Penny tiptoed the last few steps to her cabin.

Stopped in surprise. Diego Ramos waited on her porch.

"Can I help you?" She dredged up a smile.

He leapt down the steps. "What's wrong?"

"Not a thing." She continued onto her porch. Her synapses weren't firing on all cylinders because although she'd been up for hours, it was still way early. He followed. "What are you doing here?"

"Partners yoga."

Oh, God. Her shoulders slumped. There went her nap.

"Where've you been?"

"Chores at my farm." Penny rested against the front door and let her eyes drift closed. She'd promised Zinnia. "Give me a few minutes and I'll be ready to go."

What she wouldn't give for five minutes of sleep. Maybe she could fake savasana and sleep during yoga.

"What time did you get up?" He wrapped his arm around her shoulders. Dang, that felt nice.

"Umm, four-ish."

"You got two hours' sleep?"

"More or less." She might have spent a minute or twenty—before she actually slept—thinking about Diego Ramos and those kisses and what good use they could put those condoms to.

He smelled so good, like man and a hint of cologne. His stubble had grown into a thicker dusting, darkening the stark line of his jaw and emphasizing his lips. The urge to just lean on his muscled chest and close her eyes and inhale his scent snaked through her with insidious warmth.

He opened her door and half carried her inside.

"Seriously, be good to go in a sec."

"You're asleep on your feet."

Mmm. The cabin was warm and the bed beckoned like a lighthouse on the shore. Warm hands on her shoulders and then her neck. He tilted her head up. "Open your eyes."

The whispered command held a note of domination. She blearily pried open her eyelids.

"So tired." She wrapped her arms around his waist. God, he felt so good.

Solid. Warm. Masculine.

Diego snuggled her closer, until her head rested in the perfect hollow beneath his chin as if made just for her.

The cabin door closed with a loud thump, locking them inside and the rest of the world out.

The promise of sleep was fading as other impressions registered. His hard, masculine chest was solid beneath her cheek. His biceps cradled her close. The rapidly growing bulge of his erection nudged her belly.

A deep-seated, burgeoning arousal spread from her core, infusing her with a languid, intense desire. "Oh," she breathed.

And the feelings from last night, from that amazing kiss, blossomed and spread through her as she melted against him.

She wanted to jump him.

She might be reading his signals wrong. Maybe he reacted this way to any woman. But as the air between them thickened and grew, a syrupy sensual arousal spread through her. She wanted to hibernate in this cabin and have a sex marathon. Hot, sweaty, physical sex.

Her breath stuttered.

"What?"

She certainly wasn't about to confess that she'd been fantasizing about jumping him. But just thinking about them together, she was likely beet red.

"You got some sun yesterday."

"Yeah, that crazy sun." She determinedly didn't look at him as she willed herself to stop blushing.

"Or maybe you're red for another reason."

Her gaze shot to him.

He smiled, his face transformed, his mouth ticked up on one side, revealing his white teeth and hinting at a wicked streak. He knew exactly what she was thinking about. And if the hard dick prodding her abdomen was any indication, he was thinking it right back.

Lust thrummed through her.

Her defenses down, her inhibitions low, she pushed him back against the solid wood of the cabin door and kissed the underside of his jaw. "This is what I was thinking about," she said against his skin.

His arms tightened around her and he groaned.

She wanted that feeling of flying. The pure incandescence of sexual release. When was the last time she'd taken anything for just her? She'd visited Brad last night in the hospital. He hadn't left his boyfriend's side. And her second thought, after how beautiful his devotion was, if she was in an accident, no one would feel that way about her.

Was it a lack in her, or a lack of effort to find someone to share things with? Of course those thoughts took a back seat to her current obsession.

She didn't have the time to find that someone right now, but here was a guy who, based on the boner prodding her belly, was interested in connecting on a physical level. She was going to take him up on the implied offer. Grab hold of him and make the most of this opportunity because who knew when she'd have the chance for sex again.

She was too busy. Too invested in everything else in her life to have time to make room for a man, a relationship, but sex? Sex she could do.

Mesmerized, she couldn't look away. His essence wrapped around her and pulled her closer, like a tractor beam.

Her heart fluttered at how close he was with his dark hair and dark eyes and mysterious smile. She wanted to dive into that dangerous pool of attraction and drown in his sexual pull. In the hushed, intimate atmosphere of her cabin, neither said a word.

Suddenly her breath constricted. Hard to draw in enough oxygen, she huffed in air. Her heart beat harder, banging against her breastbone so loudly that she couldn't hear anything but her own labored breath.

His gaze dropped to her mouth, lingered.

Penny licked her lips in the suddenly dry air. And his gaze heated, intensified.

Diego leaned closer.

She waited, held on the precipice. Would he kiss her or back off?

And what did she want?

What she should do was skedaddle out of this cabin. But that's not what she wanted. She wanted him to kiss her.

She'd been thinking about it, and more, since their encounter on the dock during the welcome cocktail party. The yearning had only intensified after his care for Zinnia last night.

Diego Ramos was a good guy.

And it had been so very long since she'd had any guy in her life.

Penny reached out a hand, trailed her fingers along his biceps, watching the goose bumps rise on his skin as she feathered her fingertips over the muscles in his shoulder and then scraped her fingernails along his neck.

He studied her, clearly waiting to see what she'd do next. And still he didn't speak.

Penny threaded her fingers in the short hair at his nape and tugged him down to meet her lips.

He came willingly, a small smile on his mouth. His hips bumped hers, his impressive erection nudging her belly.

Her inhibitions down, and the silence weighing on her, she blurted out the first thing that popped into her head. "Is that a pickle in your pants or are you happy to see me?"

He grinned against her mouth. "Happy," he growled.

They met in the middle. The kiss was sure, warm, luscious. Crazy.

But Penny thought, not for the first time this weekend, maybe she needed a little more crazy in her life.

<hr />

GOOFY. Inappropriate. Penny's expression held a freedom Diego envied. He measured every word he uttered. Ever since he'd committed to expanding his business he'd been on guard.

He dated sophisticated, elegant women who were perfectly at home in NYC or at a Red Sox game but none of those women would have gotten their hands dirty or even thought her slightly raunchy invitation.

Her down-to-earth charm was doing it for him in a big way.

Her lips were soft and sensual. She carried the scent of fresh grass and honey.

And he wanted to eat her up.

Diego cupped her face in his palms and with the attention to detail of a traveler in a strange land, he explored her mouth.

The door was hard at his back and Penny was pressed up against him.

Lust, previously at a low simmer, exploded and accelerated like an out-of-control V-8. With the force of a .375 hemi engine and a light hand on the throttle, his body revved and shimmied.

He cupped her ass in his hands and rocked her softness against his hard cock. All pistons firing and revving to go, Diego slanted his head and dove into the suddenly carnal kiss.

The surge of lust took him by surprise. Lately he'd been a little disconnected, a little tired of the constant push for more. Right this moment he wanted to take something just for himself. To forget about the business, about his responsibilities, about all the people who depended on him, and just take.

And who he wanted to take was currently wrapped around him like a python.

He flung aside analysis and concerns and possibilities and went for it. He was spiraling into a place where stopping would be hard. He broke their kiss, needing to confirm they were on the same page. "I want you."

Her breasts were pillowed against his chest, arms tight around his neck, head tilted back so she could stare into his eyes.

Her Rallye Green gaze snagged his.

The need there nearly brought him to his knees.

"Excellent," she said huskily. "I want you too."

That was his greenlight. He dove into the kiss.

Diego licked into her mouth, her lips parted and her tongue stroked his eagerly.

The kiss rocked his world.

When he pulled away, her freckles stood out in her flushed face, and her lips were reddened. Her breath puffed against his mouth. They both waited, hesitating on the brink of a change.

She gathered her energy, as though she was going to step back. Step away.

No, he didn't want that.

His body buzzed with an excess of energy and deep well of fulfillment.

But instead of pulling away, she tugged him toward the bed.

Penny fell back onto the quilt. She parted her legs and he landed between them. Right where he wanted to be.

He propped on one elbow and skimmed his hand beneath the tails of her shirt, too impatient to unbutton the soft flannel, pushing the material up to bare her stomach. "So soft," he murmured against her ribs.

Penny burrowed her hands beneath his basketball shorts and cupped his ass. Her questing fingers scraped over his skin, and fuck but he wanted those hands somewhere else.

She rocked into his cock. "So hard."

He rolled so lay on their sides facing each other.

"Touch me," he groaned, then nipped his way up her

ribcage to her luscious breasts. They were small, perky, and begging for his mouth.

"Return the—" she gasped when his mouth closed over her pert nipple, "—favor. Oh holy manure."

He bit back a laugh.

Goofy. And still so hot. He tongued her nipple against the roof of his mouth, sucked the tight bud inside while he caressed her other breast with his fingers. She fit his hand perfectly. He squeezed. Satisfaction thrummed through him when she arched into his touch.

Penny pushed down his shorts and curled her hand around his cock. She explored him tentatively, her thumb brushing the sensitive tip.

"Harder," he begged.

He shoved her shirt over her head, exposing her breasts.

Her tan lines were sharply defined—she clearly spent a lot of time in the sun in just a bikini top. His hands were dark against the white skin of her breasts, the contrast ramping him up to another level.

"I want to devour you."

"No one is stopping you," she said breathlessly.

Diego pushed her jeans down her hips.

"Oh." Her hand gripped his wrist, his pulse thudding frantically against her rough fingertips.

"*Mierda.* You want to stop." He dropped his forehead to her shoulder, breathing deeply, trying to control his erection.

"No!" She flushed hard.

Fascinated, he watched the red spread over her chest and into her cheeks.

"Um, just don't look at my underwear. It's…not sexy."

"*Querida*, I don't give a damn about your underwear."
He shoved the plain white cotton off her hips.

He stroked his hands over her naked skin, learning her
curves, learning what made her purr. Women were like
engines—each had their own little idiosyncrasies and trigger
points. He trailed his fingers over her hips, down her thighs,
then drew his fingers up until he reached the apex of
her sex.

She jerked at the first touch of his fingers. He threaded
through her curls, found her wet, then began to tease.

But Penny paid him back in kind. One hand wrapped
around his cock, the other struggled with his ribbed tank
until he yanked it off one handed.

They were both naked now.

She scraped her fingernails at the base of his neck.
Goose bumps peppered his skin. His balls tightened up, his
body more than ready to take the plunge. Within seconds
they'd gone from zero to sixty.

"Now," she panted.

Shit. "Condom." He didn't have one.

She started laughing. The sound shifted something in
his heart.

"Don't think it's that funny."

"My own sex god." She laughed even harder, tears
leaking from her eyes.

She arched beneath him, her breasts pushed up into his
face and he bent to suck a still-hard nipple into his mouth.
She extended her arm to the little night table, moaning as
he sucked harder.

She pulled open the drawer of the nightstand.

"Can't reach." She gestured to the bedside table.

He reached into the drawer and grabbed some packages. In his fist were several but the one that caught his eye was white with a familiar red cross.

He squinted. "Orgasm Donor," was printed underneath the red cross symbol.

He suppressed a snort. "I'm happy to donate some orgasms to your cause," he teased. Then his brain stumbled on that thought. She had condoms.

Thank God, because his cock had not gotten the message that stopping was imminent.

She had condoms.

She grabbed one from his fist and tossed the others onto the quilt. "Got it!" she said in triumph and waved the little packet in his face.

He rolled them again, so Penny was on top.

She took the latex and proceeded to sheath him.

He should slow it down, make her beg, make her moan, but she knelt over him, knees on the outside of his hips.

Like a goddess, her head thrown back, the tip of her braids brushed his thighs. Her pert breasts were pink with beard burn and her nipples wet from his mouth. The pagan goddess pose did it for him.

Arms filled with sexy woman and his cock covered and ready to go. Diego abandoned his thoughts of tasting her all over. Next time.

He cupped her hips in his palms and guided her onto his cock. So full he could burst, he wanted to move. But he held back, letting her sink onto his erection at her own pace, knowing once she started moving, he wouldn't last long.

Once she was fully seated, her sex gloved him, her ass on

his thighs, she tilted her head and met his gaze with glassy green eyes.

"Okay?" he asked.

"More than." Her smile was a little wicked and a lot aroused. Then Penny began to rock into him. Every downward stroke her sex squeezed his cock. "Harder," she demanded.

Diego grabbed her hips and thrust up. She threw her head back as they slammed together. Once they found a rhythm, the intensity increased. His cock was harder than steel as he pistoned his hips. With every thrust, her small breasts bounced.

Winded and flushed, Penny bent over him, her nipple even with his mouth. He craned his neck and sucked her inside. The change in angle was the trigger. With every thrust he rubbed the head of his cock against her G-spot, the bundle of nerves swelled and her body began to buck against his.

Her fists clenched against his shoulders, and her thighs tightened around his hips with each cataclysmic coming together, until Penny gave a cry, arching back. Her body tightened around him as her orgasm spread over her face. Her sex clamped around his cock, milking him. His balls tightened, and energy pooled at the base of his spine until he catapulted over the edge.

His vision whited out, sparklers flickering behind his closed eyelids as his body exploded. His come shot into the condom in intense jerks.

His heart thundered in his chest, as he stared up at the woman who tempted him to break his long held rules. Sweat gleamed on her skin, and her eyes were closed as pleasure waterfalled over her face.

With an oomph, Penny fell facedown on him. Diego shifted so Penny sprawled over top of him, and his cock loved the Penny blanket.

Did she just…fall asleep on him?

Her breath snuffled softly against his neck. She had.

How tired was she that she crashed on his shoulder? Wasn't the guy the one who was supposed to fall asleep after sex? Diego huffed out a laugh.

His heart still thundered, and his body was still buzzing with the aftermath of explosive sex. Goddamn, he'd needed that. The grinding pain in his stomach had all but gone. His shoulders were more relaxed than they had been in months.

Sated, content, he wrapped his arm around her back and held her to him. She felt profoundly right in his arms. For a moment, he didn't want to let her go.

He definitely didn't want to wake her up. Two hours' sleep? After the day she'd had yesterday, and their energetic round of sex, no wonder she was dead on her feet. And no way was he forcing her to go to partners yoga. He'd face Zinnia's wrath. "Sweetheart. What time do you have to have to get up?"

"Kayak races at umm, nine."

"Sleep. I'll make sure you're awake."

She nuzzled his neck, pressed a kiss to his skin. The innocent touch buzzed through him and his dick, the bastard, got hard again.

She muttered something that might have been "Thanks."

As if his reassurance popped the release on her restraint, her body went liquid, turning into a limp noodle.

Her chest expanded and contracted against his as she slept deeply. Her lips puffed breath against his neck, raising goose bumps and spreading tingles more across his naked flesh.

She was out.

Diego curled his arms around her body and rolled them onto their sides. He took care of the condom without shifting her from beneath his arm and then relaxed onto the mattress. He should get up, tuck her in, and leave. Staying around after release wasn't usually his thing, but he didn't want to wake her. So he set the alarm button on his watch, giving her a little bit of snooze time, and shifted her so that her head rested in the crook of his neck.

She threw one bare leg over his and her hand skimmed down his stomach, resting near his groin.

His heart thudded beneath her cheek, booming so hard he was afraid he might wake her up. But instead she settled closer, and curled her fingers against his naked skin. When was the last time he'd just hung out with a woman?

Usually he was too busy. Had too many meetings and action items taking up his day to relax. He was either working, working out, or sleeping. But now he was trapped on the relatively comfortable bed, arms full of sexy woman, and nowhere to go. The warm cabin, the female full of soft curves and sweet sighs, and his general fatigue all caught up with him.

His last cogent thought was Zin was going to kill him.

But what a way to go.

❦ 8 ❦

Penny was cocooned, enveloped and warmed by a band across her lower back. She didn't want to wake up but someone's annoying alarm wouldn't shut up.

God, she wanted to sink back into sleep for about a hundred years.

Her bed felt weird. Not bad, nice actually, but weird. A steady thump echoed in her ears as she snuggled closer. "Just five more minutes," she murmured. Like she could talk the alarm into snoozing.

But the irritating beep kept going.

Her bed rumbled, then let out a very masculine groan. *What?!*

That shock to the system had her jerking awake. Then her solid bed began to move. Penny clung tight and opened her eyes. Holy manure, she was nearly lying on top of Diego Ramos.

She was still naked.

And she'd had sex with him. Images and sensations rushed back in.

She'd had amazing sex with him. And oh my God, she had not intended to fall asleep on him.

His firm hand pressed against her lower back as he reached for something. He'd kept his arms wrapped tight around her while asleep.

Umm, what just happened?

Diego thunked his head onto the pillow. Her heart threatened to thunder out of her chest. His very hard, very impressive erection pulsed against her hip. Very big. Penny went a little lightheaded remembering that thick invasion and the resulting orgasm.

Jesus, she was a nympho. But before this morning, she hadn't had sex in…when had she and her ex called it quits? Months ago, last summer maybe.

"I, you're um, up, I mean, I should get up…." Oh God. She dropped her head against his shoulder and hid from his gaze. "I need to go."

He chuckled.

It really wasn't that funny.

She lifted her head and glared at him.

"We're both up." His grin was a little crooked and a lot mischievous. His brown eyes sparkled with wicked intent.

"Not helping."

She should get up, but she held still for one more second, enjoying the hard male body against her and the way his cock pulsed against her lower belly, in time with the thud of his heart.

Penny carefully extricated from his loose embrace, her face surely a fiery red.

Diego curled to sitting, rubbed his hands over his face.

"You sort of passed out on top of me." His grin told her he hadn't minded. Completely unconcerned that he was naked as a jay, whereas Penny wanted to clutch the covers to her chest like a Victorian heroine.

"I'm quite sorry." She flushed again.

"Don't be." Diego slid closer. "I enjoyed it."

Everything came rushing back into her consciousness. She'd been so tired. Nothing embarrassing about passing out on top of a stranger. Could you call someone you were naked with a stranger?

Even though Penny hadn't seen him in twenty years, he'd been a constant presence in her life, like her conscience. She'd taken that angry boy's words to heart and learned about the rest of the world outside her insular wealthy life.

Sure the first thing that surprised her about his speech was the fact that not everyone got a new car on their birthday, but later other things had registered. People went to bed hungry.

Those simple, matter-of-fact words had changed the trajectory of her life.

Because she couldn't imagine it. Each step on her journey had been formed by that interaction.

Maybe she hadn't even realized how much impact that conversation had on her life until now.

"You okay?" He was looking at her strangely. But he was so close, his sexuality shoved out the little trip through her memories and motivation.

Naked, his warm body still pressed against hers, she knew they needed to get up and move. This little bubble was absent of tension and expectation. She'd stopped living her life to please others years ago. Now she only pleased herself.

Stupid to be shy now, but there it was. "Sure." She avoided his gaze.

She was like a nerdy schoolgirl who'd lost her tongue around the super popular quarterback. His wicked grin caught her by surprise. Except that she could almost guarantee that he'd been more likely to be bad boy behind the bleachers than on the field.

"But I need to change."

"Who's stopping you?"

No embarrassment for this guy. His gaze heated, skimmed down her body again. The room was laden with suddenly simmering lust. He was gorgeous. All dark skin and lean muscles. His cock had begun to lengthen the longer he stared at her.

She mentally shrugged. Might as well own it. Who knew when she'd have an experience like this again.

Penny stroked her palm over his shoulder, tracing the swell of his biceps and the corded lean strength of his forearm. "Thanks for the morning pick-me-up and the nap."

He laughed, his teeth white in his tan face. "Much better than partners yoga."

"Definitely more cardio than spiritual."

"I disagree. I'm pretty sure I saw heaven."

The pleasure that flowed through her filled a hole she hadn't even known existed. It was probably a line, and still she fell for it.

He leaned in and brushed a soft kiss against her mouth. His watch beeped again.

"Great way to start the day. But if we're late for the kayak races, Zin will have my ass." He leisurely picked up his shorts and tank top. "I'll wait outside."

"Not necessary. I can get to the dock."

After Diego gently closed the door, Penny quickly tugged on a string bikini, a pair of cutoffs, and a tank top imprinted with "Farmer. Because Food Producing Bad Ass was not an official job title."

Sure enough, Diego was waiting on her porch. The employee cabin was far enough away from the water that only flickers of light from the sun glinting off the lake penetrated into the woods.

They walked toward the dock in companionable silence. The mood between them surprisingly easy and not at all awkward.

When they got to the dock, a crowd had already gathered. "I need to check in with Tegan—she's taking over for Heather as camp director—and find out where she needs me. Thank you."

Now it was awkward. Should she shake his hand? Tell him he'd been an amazing orgasm donor? Let him know she'd be up for sharing a cabin again?

"My pleasure." His husky voice skimmed over her nerve endings like the rasp of sandpaper over unfinished wood.

Penny suppressed a shiver. "Good luck on your race." She hurried away, pretending, at least to herself, that she wasn't figuratively running.

Zinnia rested in an Adirondack chair along the shoreline with her booted foot propped on another chair, clipboard in her lap and megaphone in her hand. "Okay, everyone! Line up with your partners and then the camp staff will get you in your doubles kayak. We set up pairs with one member from Ramos Classic and one from London Automotive."

Penny smiled at the groans and cheers from the crowd as she headed toward Tegan. "What's my assignment?"

"Ramos and Sherry," Zinnia yelled, interrupting her conversation with Tegan.

Diego and a pretty young woman with a sparkle in her eye walked over to the waiting kayaks.

Penny didn't like the hard zing of jealousy that burned beneath her ribs. A. It was a business event. B. She had no claim on him. C. What the hell was her problem?

But that spurt of irritation didn't fade as the girl chatted animatedly with Diego.

"London and Hastings," Zin shouted out.

Penny jerked. She was supposed to race?

"That's it." Tegan smiled. "Michael asked that you accommodate Diego Ramos's company whenever needed. Although he doesn't think that they would sue, since Zinnia fell on Camp Firefly Falls property he wants to do everything possible to make sure they're happy."

Reluctantly, Penny made her way to the lake shore. The humidity had not even reached maximum capacity but still little hairs had started to curl around her face.

Jeffrey London stared at her, his distaste clearly communicated as he bent toward Diego and whispered in his ear. Diego blinked, his expression not changing as his gaze shot to her. But somehow Penny knew he was not happy.

"Change of plans," Diego's deep voice reverberated. "Jeffrey and his assistant will row together and I'll pair up with Ms. Hastings."

Penny's stomach churned.

London had refused to work with her. It was a stupid fucking camp event. She pasted a smile on her face placed a quick hand on Zinnia's shoulder. "Hope you're feeling better today. Let me know if there's anything I can do."

Zinnia shot her a grateful smile. "Thank you. Right now the pain pills are keeping me feeling fine. Just keep your promise."

To make sure Diego did his partner stuff.

She'd already partnered with Diego Ramos and it had been fabulous. She pictured his body moving aggressively inside hers, pushing her toward one more peak. Giving her more pleasure than she'd experienced in months.

Bad Penny, having sexual daydreams about her partner.

After they were outfitted with life jackets and seated in the kayak, a camp employee pushed them into the lake. Diego nodded at London.

"On your mark, get set, go!" Tegan used the megaphone to start the race.

Penny and Diego set out. The finish line was across the lake at an additional picnic area where snacks and drinks would be served.

Their paddling was out of rhythm and they listed drunkenly from left to right, not making much forward progress. Within a few minutes they lagged far behind London and his perky assistant.

Penny tried to take the lead at the same time as Diego. As a result, they were limping along behind his competitor. Not that she cared.

"What does London have against you?" He was behind her but there was no mistaking the animosity in Diego's voice. The sweet teasing guy who'd woken her up this morning was nowhere to be found.

"I have no idea." *Really*. But he definitely did.

Diego stopped paddling. "There must be something."

Her tension rose. The sick feeling in her stomach from the condemnation in Jeffrey London's gaze hadn't abated. If anything, it had gotten worse.

Thunk. Her paddle hit the water at the wrong angle, the contact zinging up her arm.

Maybe her parents' sins were again coming back to haunt her. There were those who blamed Penny. After all, her parents had skipped the country with other people's money. She was an easy target.

The Brahmin crowd didn't have any sympathy for the kid who'd been left behind and she'd been publicly vilified on a regular basis until she'd left for college. But people had long memories.

"He hates you."

She stiffened her shoulders. She'd given up caring what other people thought of her. They made up their minds no matter what the facts were.

"I want to know who I slept with," he practically hissed.

She turned around to stare at him. He was legit angry at her right now. "You're mad at *me*?"

She wanted to blast him, her temper rising. It didn't happen often. She'd had to learn to control it when she'd been attacked verbally for her parents' crimes because most of the time the bully just wanted a reaction from her. To make her cry or run away.

Right now she wouldn't cry and she couldn't run away.

"I'm mad at myself. I know better. I don't do random,

spontaneous sex." His voice was tight, annoyed, and low. "I still want to know who I accidentally slept with."

"Accidentally?" Penny officially lost her shit. But she did it quietly. "It's not like you *accidentally* slipped and put your dick in me."

She whirled back around and began paddling furiously. One side, then the other.

The beard burn on her chest tingled as if taunting her with her poor choice in lovers. But that tingle just made her more angry.

He was mad because he slept with her. Lovely.

"You want to know why he hates me." Her arms ached at the drag of the lake on the blade of the paddle. "Probably because when I was seventeen my parents fled the country with a whole bunch of people's money. And no one believed that I didn't know where they went."

"Penny," he said softly.

"So I became the public face of their crimes." Penny continued to dig through the water. "And certain groups of people have long memories. I'm guessing that he believes I'm somehow tainted by illegality."

"*Mierda.*"

"There you have it." *Dick.* But she'd promised Zinnia, so she sucked it up and said, "We need to get in sync."

Diego's paddle hit her in the head.

"Ow."

"Sorry." Diego sounded like he meant it but too little too late.

And maybe he only meant about the whack with the paddle.

"You okay?"

"I'm a lot tougher than I look." She dismissed him. The sooner they got to the other side, the sooner she could get away from him. "But we've got to get into a rhythm or Jeffrey London is going to beat you."

Diego leaned forward. The kayak rocked dangerously. "I don't care."

"Sure you do," she argued. "No one gets to be as successful as you without being competitive."

She'd just given away that she knew something about his business, about him.

"Tell me more."

"I'm assuming," she muttered. Lie.

"So you've read about me, my company?"

"I might have seen an article about you a few years ago." She'd been impressed.

"Did you deliberately attempt to sabotage my business relationship?"

What? And yes, this is what she got for simply engaging in casual sex. Nothing about her life had been casual. Why had she even tried? Life seemed to backfire on her on a regular basis.

"Self-absorbed much?" She rolled her eyes. "With your semi-charmed life, even if my taint rubbed off, you'd be fine."

He snorted. "Hard work, babe. Nothing semi-charmed about it."

As if she didn't know anything about hard work. Well, fuck him. Oh, yeah, she already did that and look how well it turned out?

They both rowed faster. "Hard work and innovation.

Yeah, how to turn failure into success," she snarled, too pissed to be diplomatic.

"It's an excellent motto," he said gruffly.

She couldn't see his face but she could hear the discomfort in his voice.

"I'm aware." She remembered the moment he'd thrown that back at her. Remembered the teenage anguish that he'd played off when he thought she was saying that he was a failure. That moment in the parking lot was indelibly imprinted on her mind. Apparently his too.

She waited to see if he would acknowledge that his motto came from her. From that stupid naïve kid she'd been.

But he was quiet.

They rowed faster. Now that they were in sync, they were making forward progress. They were almost caught up to London and his assistant. "You going to back off or are you going to let him win?"

And goddamn, did she want Jeffrey London to lose. Because of course she hadn't had sex with Diego in the hopes of some grand love that would last until the end of time—dramatic much?—but she had hoped for more than that one quick bang in the cabin.

What she hadn't anticipated was being accused of trying to damage his business deal. The ass.

The sooner they got to the finish line, the sooner she would have fulfilled her obligation to Zinnia and she could get away from Diego Ramos.

Screw him. Not literally, obviously. That was over. Never again.

9

Diego stalked toward the next activity.

Lunch with Jeffrey London had been strained, only becoming easier when the conversation turned to business.

He hadn't spoken with Penny since she took off after the kayak race. He could have handled that better. Okay, honesty time, he couldn't have handled it much worse.

Remorse and a sick shame slithered through him.

He knew what it was like to be judged on your parents' mistakes. Before he'd gone to live with Tío Raul permanently, he'd borne the brunt of other people's judgment for his parent's bad choices. What happened twelve years ago and Jeffrey London's reaction to her all these years later meant the scandal must have been intense.

So yeah, he sucked.

But, *Cristo*, having sex with her had put a crimp in his dealings with London.

He should never have deviated from his typical mode of choosing sexual partners for business reasons. His usual partners were elegant, well-connected, and chosen for whatever benefit they could bring to his business or social standing. Sure, his dating process was a little cold but everything in his life revolved around building his business and promoting his brand so he could ascend to the next level.

That method was a hell of a lot smarter than because he had a hard-on. He'd been shrewd about sexual partners for fifteen years.

And look what happened when he disregarded his personal commandments just once.

He'd hurt her feelings. He was sorry. But this weekend was all about seeing if his business practices and leadership style were compatible with London's. The last thing he should do was hook up with a woman Jeffrey London hated.

London had spent lunch criticizing Penny Hastings.

Diego had gotten a polite diatribe, vitriolic for all its quiet upper crust wording, about the evil, immoral, unethical dealings of the Hastings family.

He'd wanted to defend Penny but he didn't. He justified his silence by telling himself he didn't really know what happened. And he had people depending on him—his employees and family all had a stake in making this venture work. His whole life was on the line.

Even if the sex had been fantastic, he couldn't afford to blow this deal.

Every move and counter move was a negotiation step in the dance to merge with London Automotive.

Which was why he'd gotten his shit together and gotten in sync with Penny for the kayak race. Diego and Penny had managed to tie with London and his assistant, crossing the finish line at the same time.

As soon as they hit the shore, Penny had exited the kayak and headed toward the picnic tables. Diego was left to hand off the kayak and make small talk with London while the rest of their employees finished their races.

For some reason, Diego was hyper-aware of Penny at all times. And he knew exactly when she'd left the area.

He needed to apologize.

And he would as soon as he found her. But right now he was on his way to the Nature Walk Bingo event. Someone from the camp had placed a folding chair at the entrance to the hiking path and the woods. Zin sat like a queen on her throne, handing out printed bingo cards and a plastic bag that held a small grease pencil stapled to the back of the paper.

"We're going to have the cards for the duration of the retreat. We're using the honor system and you can mark off your own squares. After the cook-off tomorrow night, we'll be awarding prizes. So don't lose it!"

Zin's infuriated gaze promised retribution. "Play nice," she whispered as she shoved the card into his hand.

He made small talk with his friends and employees. Raul Jr. grinned before giving his sister a kiss on the cheek. London's assistant, Sherry, scurried up the path from the cabins. Her hair was a little mussed. "Mr. London got an unexpected business call. He sends his regrets."

Well, that was a lie.

If he wasn't mistaken, London had been having an old-fashioned nooner with Sherry.

But before he could reflect any further, Penny strode up to the waiting group.

"Good afternoon, everyone!" She smiled brightly at the group but studiously avoided Diego's gaze. "My name is Penny Hastings and I'll be your nature guide for the afternoon."

She'd changed from earlier. She wore cutoff jeans shorts, another skimpy tank top with the Camp Firefly Falls logo that clung tightly to her breasts, and what seemed to be her ubiquitous plaid flannel, this time tied at her waist. She had on sturdy, well-worn hiking boots and socks that puffed above the top of the boots, accenting her gorgeous tanned legs. The same ones he'd had wrapped around him as he powered inside her this morning.

Shit. Off-limits. In more than one way.

Penny had put on some makeup and carried a small backpack with a water bottle clipped to the side. She'd also plopped a green bucket hat over her braids. She gestured to the cooler next to Zinnia. "Everyone make sure to grab a bottle of water before we get started."

Zin sat in the chair with a cookie and a glass of water watching intently. "Check your sheet for your hiking partner. Everyone needs a buddy. Camp rules."

Diego hadn't paid much attention to the paper Zin had handed him. He looked now and realized he was paired with Penny again.

Which brought out conflicting feelings. But mostly happiness. He needed to apologize. But didn't really want to do it in public.

"Oh, since Jeffrey isn't here, and you're incapacitated, I

can partner with Mr. Ramos." Sherry smiled brightly, her gaze a tad too avaricious for him.

"I guess that will work since Penny is leading the hike now." Zin's reluctant frown indicated how she felt about it.

"Our schedule changed a bit due to some unforeseen circumstances," Penny said to the group at large. "Initially we were going to have an informational session about the future of corporate gardens and then you were going to do your hike with Heather, but she has fallen ill so we decided to combine the two."

"We didn't really come here for that type of thing." Sherry all but sneered.

Penny's smile didn't change but beneath her hat, her green eyes narrowed. "Well, you get a twofer today. Aren't you lucky?" she chirped.

Her smile said if she could strangle Sherry with that luck, she'd be a lot happier.

"She's lucky Jeff isn't here, that's for sure," Sherry muttered.

Penny began walking backward so she could face the group. All the employees were slated for this event, then for late afternoon they had free time with offerings of ziplining, an arts-and-crafts session, or plain old lazing by the lake.

Raul came hurrying up to Diego's side. "Hey. Apparently my partner has sunstroke so you two get me." He turned his considerable charm on Sherry who glanced between them, looking as if she'd won the lottery.

When Sherry stumbled, Raul linked his arm with hers. "To help you stay steady on your feet."

She shot him a grateful smile. "Thanks."

Penny lectured the group. "As we go along, I'll point out

the flora and fauna native to the Berkshires. We live in a very ecologically significant place. You can also follow along on your bingo card. Each card has some squares with pictures of a tree, plant, bird, or wildlife we might see on the trail."

And so they set off. Most of Diego's employees had gotten into the spirit and clutched the bingo card in one hand while they watched Penny and listened. London's employees as a whole definitely weren't as interested.

Sherry chattered at Raul. In fact, she never shut up, completely ignoring Penny's trail guide lecture. So Diego subtly moved away from the pair, drawn forward by the lilting music of Penny Hasting's voice.

She gestured to various plants and birds as they walked along the gently upward sloping upward path. He could admit that he preferred her on her back crying out his name, to this crowd of people who were keeping her from him.

Not that she'd have anything to do with him.

Not that he should have anything to do with her. She could completely fuck up his deal with London Automotive.

Penny continued. "While we're hiking into the interior of the woods, let me tell you a bit about corporate gardens and why they're a good idea."

For the next twenty minutes, Diego listened to Penny talk about her corporate garden project. Her enthusiasm for the project was contagious, and soon employees from both companies were asking specific, logistical questions about the idea.

Alma, his human resources manager, wove between the pairs of employees to approach Diego. Her hands were clasped tightly like she was praying. "I want to do this."

"Now isn't the time to discuss it." But he smiled, letting her know they would talk about it later. Although he was already leaning toward the idea, they needed hard data and fiscal costs before they could move forward.

Sherry interrupted their conversation. "No way will Jeff, um, Mr. London go for that." She shook her head, the silky blond curls brushing her shoulders. "He's all about the bottom line. He fired his brother-in-law last year because he was abusing the company credit card."

Her eyes rounded, she placed her palm over her mouth, her pink fingernails shiny and perfect. "Forget I said that."

For some reason, he flashed back to Penny's short unpainted nails, her hand wrapped around his cock as she pumped him. And shit, not the place to go right now.

"This is just a first intro. Nothing is off the table for CAR yet," Diego said.

Alma rolled her eyes. "Thanks, Diego."

"Oh! Look!" Penny paused on the trail.

Cristo, she sounded just like she had when she'd come on his cock this morning.

Diego had a hard-on. He hoped no one was paying attention.

"See this bird here. That's a blackpoll warbler! She's not on the card because she's difficult to spot." Her voice was light, her smile wide. "This is a rare treat. And since we found her, you can mark the more common raven off on your card."

She paused so everyone could get out their pencil and X out the bird. Diego handed their bag to Raul. Unbidden, his gaze kept returning to Penny. Diego's mind wandered to when he'd been inside her. Her sleek legs were bare. He wanted those legs wrapped around his hips, heels digging into his ass.

She had removed her flannel and tied the arms around her waist. He could see the light green scalloped lace straps of her bra. Fancier than her white cotton from this morning. He could give a fuck what her underwear looked like, but he was man enough to admit that the green lace was more intriguing.

The tank top dipped low enough to give a peek at the shadowed valley between her breasts and slightly reddened skin—likely from his beard. He had the inappropriate urge to find out if her panties matched that very feminine lace. Chances of that happening were less than zero. She was still pissed at him.

As she should be.

Penny pointed to another tree, explaining the characteristics of the leaves. But his brain focused on the defined muscles in her arms. An army-green bucket hat covered her rich auburn hair, shaded her face, and gave her an impish appeal. Her face glistened with a slight sheen of sweat from the exertion of the hike.

A ray of sunlight speared through a break in the canopy and highlighted her eyes, and the mesmerizing forest echoed back in her gaze, seemingly lit from within.

She'd kept up a vigorous pace while they hiked through the woods. "Make sure not to stray too far off the path. The groomed trails are to keep the rest of the forest as natural as possible."

They stopped regularly so she could point out balsam fir

needles, sugar maple leaves, and wild blueberry brambles, and then mark them off on their cards. The group was able to X off various items on the bingo cards as they spied them on the hike.

A loamy decay of dropped leaves and the damp from last week's rain scented the air. Musical birds twittered and small animals chattered in the lush greenery of the woods surrounding the hikers.

During the hike Diego had moved through the crowd as more people lagged behind, needing to be closer to her. Like a magnet pulled toward metal, he couldn't ignore the draw of her personality.

A frog croaked, and Sherry shrieked.

"That's just a bullfrog. At the lower elevations, during spring the wetlands flood, creating vernal pools which are breeding grounds for all sorts of amphibians." Penny's gaze sparkled with mirth. "So if you see a salamander or newt in your cabin, just open the door and let the little guy out."

"Oh my God." Sherry pranced on the trail like she was terrified of a frog.

Diego caught the evil twinkle in Penny's smile. "Don't worry, they don't bite."

When Sherry squealed and ran back the way they came. Diego jerked his head at Raul telling him to go after the annoying assistant. Raul sighed, mouthed, "You owe me," and followed the overly excitable woman.

Penny switched back to explaining the benefits of her corporate farming project, finishing with the option to give the food to the local food bank. "Any questions?"

Alma raised her hand.

"Alma, you don't have to raise your hand, we're informal here."

"What made you envision this program and giving back to food pantries?"

"Good question." Penny laughed. "When I was a kid it never occurred to me that other kids went to bed hungry…" she trailed off.

If he hadn't been explicitly watching her, he might have missed the guilty little jerk of her gaze away from him.

Penny smiled wistfully, "Then one day, someone made me realize that I was pretty lucky."

Diego nearly stumbled. Was she talking about him?

She shrugged. "When I was in Ag school we had a final project that involved giving back to the community. And I conceived the idea for *FEED Together*. I've been dreaming about implementing this for years."

"Well, I think it's a great idea," Alma praised.

Penny's smile lit up her whole face. "Me too."

They continued to tromp along the trail with the group asking questions and Penny answering, while pointing out flora and fauna.

But Diego only half-listened, his mind back on the confrontation they'd had twenty years ago.

Apparently he wasn't the only one who'd had his world view changed all those years ago. That blew his mind. He'd never even considered that his rant in the parking lot had made an impression on her.

10

Thank the full harvest moon that was over.

The mood among the group she'd led along the trail had been a mix of annoyance and interest. Now the campers were headed off to zipline or make crafts or just hang by the lake, and Penny had a few hours free before she had to help serve dinner.

She plopped down on the folding chair someone had put at the trailhead for Zinnia. She'd kept her promise to Michael Tully, and now thankfully Diego Ramos seemed to have disappeared. He had sent her smoldering looks all through the hike.

Mixed signals much?

After judging her because of Jeffrey London's bias this morning, he'd ignored her at lunch.

She should still be mad at him. But if she was honest, she was hurt more than angry. However he seemed open to her corporate farming project so she couldn't afford to piss him off. And damn him, he'd certainly looked sexy during the bingo hike.

The walkie-talkie at her hip squawked. "Penny, can you check the trail to make sure no one got lost?" Tegan requested.

Penny wanted to roll her eyes. "Who'm I looking for?"

"*Mister* London is looking for his assistant."

"She ran back the way we started when we heard a frog."

Tegan snorted.

They weren't supposed to laugh at the guests. Of course they weren't. But Penny laughed anyway. She wasn't an employee of the camp, and *Mister* London's assistant had been completely rude while Penny had been speaking. She'd talked through her entire speech. "Apparently, she's not really a nature girl."

"Make sure she isn't lost on the trail?"

"Sure." Penny pushed to her feet. She'd really been hoping for a nap.

Diego jogged up beside her, looking far better than any guy had a right to. "I'll come with you."

How did he know where she was going? "Not necessary." Her tone was clipped.

He sidled closer to her. "Didn't you emphasize the buddy system before our hike?" His words puffed against her neck. A chill shivered over her skin and peppered her arms with goose bumps.

She flushed. "Fine."

They retraced the hike from the beginning. Penny walked briskly, trying to race through the re-walk. She doubted Sherry was still on the trail. The faster she got through this, the faster she could ditch one Diego Ramos.

"How old were you when you discovered kids didn't always have three meals and a snack every day?"

Nine years and nine months old. Near this very spot. Fudge. She did not want to talk about this. She kept walking, now practically sprinting. "Ten? Eleven? I don't remember."

"Bullshit."

She jerked to a stop. "What?"

"You know exactly when."

Not touching that one. "What do you care?"

After all, he was the one who'd judged and juried her when it became apparent that Jeffrey London had a problem with her very existence.

She wanted to hold on to that resentment. Yet, she had to play nice because based on what Alma Fuentes had relayed, she was very interested in being one of Penny's first customers.

"What I meant to say was, I have high hopes for the program starting a movement." She kept her tone even and her words measured. But she didn't look at him.

She was doing a decent job of masking her frustration. But she seesawed between her passion and commitment to this project and her conflicted emotions after sleeping with him and then getting rejected. Ugh. It had been years since she worried about her reactions and her words. She'd left all that behind, and yet here she was. But the project was worth her hurt feelings and having to hold in a few choice words.

"Penny." Diego grabbed her hand. Halted her in her tracks.

His hand was solid, a little rough, as he curled his fingers around hers. She remembered him cupping her face so very gently. All those lovely pheromones flooded her body, lighting up her nerve endings and fizzing through her bloodstream.

"Yeah?" she rasped.

He tugged her around so she faced him.

His dark eyes were serious, his expression gentle. "I think it's a great idea."

Warmth flooded her, filling her heart with an unexpected joy. "Oh, well, thanks. Me too." She stumbled through gratitude.

He stood strong and resolute. The forest was alive with the clicks and clacks and chirps of birds and squirrels. Dappled sunlight hid and revealed his heated expression.

They were probably the only humans around for several miles.

If this were a Disney movie, this would be the moment when the birds and wildlife fluttered around the couple and dropped a crown of flowers on their heads, singing while the characters kissed and the music crescendoed.

In the hushed air, anticipation shimmered between them.

Her heart thudded in her ears, drowning out the sounds of the forest. Her blood slowed, chugging when instead of letting her go, he stepped closer.

She was mad at him. Wasn't she? She still wasn't quite over the accidentally-slept-with comment.

And he was mad at her. Illogically, she might add. Wasn't he?

Diego tipped his head. His hand came up, his thumb caressing her cheek.

"What—" she said faintly "—was that for?"

"You had a smudge of dirt on your cheekbone."

"Oh, um, thanks." Penny flushed. She always seemed to be dirty around him.

"For how perfectly pristine you were as a kid, you certainly have changed," he murmured.

There was a subject she'd rather avoid.

"Why the face?"

"I was expected to stay clean, perfect." And yeah, a psychologist would probably have a field day with her obstinate refusal to adhere to those expectations anymore. Her parents had insisted Penny always be above reproach, clean, put together, not a speck of dirt anywhere. Her resentment at their standards bubbled through her. "Apparently, embezzling money wasn't a problem as long as the Hastings' appearance standards were met." Her bitterness seeped into her words.

She hadn't heard from her parents in over eleven years. You'd think she'd be over it.

She was mostly resigned to the fact that her parents were assholes. But sometimes she still wanted to scream about it.

DIEGO STUDIED HER. "Didn't mean to bring up a painful subject." His missed her earlier joy. She'd been animated, happy, while wandering through the woods and teaching the crowd about nature. His careless observance had smothered that delight.

She shrugged. His palms slid over her sun-warmed skin. The scent of coconut and bug spray mingled with something floral. "It's a fact of life." But she grimaced. "But they aren't here to release my frustration on, so sometimes I let my abandonment issues get the better of me."

"You never heard from them again?" Her parents had left her alone to face the scandal?

"Nope." Penny closed her eyes and tilted her face toward the sun. The muted rays filtered through the canopy of trees. The expression on her face had relaxed into her normal cheerfulness. "What can you do? You go on."

He had so many questions, but she had exuded a peaceful, natural vibe, until she talked about her parents. And he wanted to bring back that joy.

Diego rubbed his jaw. The slight dusting of stubble was now the full-on beginnings of a beard. He should probably shave. But he found the texture beneath his hand soothed him.

She inhaled deeply and he tried, he really did, not to notice how her breasts lifted. And he remembered how she'd filled his hands.

She didn't need him creeping on her right now.

A smile spread over her upturned face. "I can seriously hear you thinking right now."

"Hopefully not completely." The unfiltered words tumbled out, surprising him. He never spoke without thinking first.

She laughed, and opened her bright green eyes. "Inappropriate?"

"Maybe."

Her smile was contagious, and Diego smiled back.

"As much as you're giving me a hard time about changing, you're a lot different than you were as a kid."

He was curious what she'd thought of him. "How so?"

"You're very…focused."

He could be. Lust simmered between them.

"What I remember about that summer is how angry you were."

True.

"Now you're so…."

He raised an eyebrow.

"Respectable." She snorted.

Diego had worked his ass off to become a respected businessman. He made all the right connections, dated all the right women, contributed to all the right causes. Every single decision he'd made since finding the breakfast club had been geared toward success. "I try." And yet, he'd thrown that all to the wind when he'd had sex with her without vetting her. So unlike him. "And yet, I am still impulsive on occasion."

"Turning a negative into a positive?" She waited.

"About that." He cleared his throat. "I'm sorry."

She blinked, tilted her head, assessed him. "For what?"

Shit. This was a frickin' minefield. He knew it and yet he could only answer one way. "For yelling at you all those years ago."

She flicked her hand. "I was a spoiled b—"

"Baby." He finished before she could. "You were a child. And I never should have yelled at you."

She shrugged, a half lift of one shoulder. "We both got over it."

"That is true," Diego said. "But I should also thank you."

"Thank me?"

"You opened my eyes to another way of looking at life."

"Same."

That regretful lump that settled in his breastbone whenever he thought about their clash dissolved, just flowed away like oil into the garage drain.

Before he could tell her how profoundly grateful he was for that confrontation, she beat him to it.

"I wouldn't be where I am today if you hadn't made me see the world differently."

Well.

Her look was provocative. And that joy was back. She wasn't mad anymore. And that he was able to prod her out of that mood sparked something in him. A little pop of satisfaction his chest puffed with a weirdly inordinate pride. He'd done that.

They stood in the middle of the forest, staring at each other.

The moment was fraught with an importance that suffused them both. Diego edged closer to Penny. The burden of that weight now gone, he was lighter, more hopeful.

In the hushed forest, the only sound was their breathing. A thick soup of regret and gratitude and relief and joy simmered in the air around them. Those emotions morphed, and the attraction that they'd managed to suppress roared back to life.

"So that's how you ended up as CEO of your own company?"

"Well, there were a lot of factors, but it all started when you opened my eyes to possibilities."

"That's a nice way of couching my naïveté."

"Maybe. But you also didn't think twice about believing that I could become more."

"More what?"

"More than I was. That started my journey."

"That's still a pretty big leap between a kid who needed a new whatever car part, and CEO," Penny said, prodding him to tell his story.

"I always thought I'd be able to apologize to you later," Diego said.

"It's later." She smirked.

"The next summer," he clarified. "But I ended up learning how to fix cars in my uncle's shop instead."

"Zinnia's dad?"

"Yep. And Raul's."

"You still haven't explained how you got from there to here."

"About six years later I was trying to sneak into a seminar for young entrepreneurs—"

"Really?"

"Yeah." He ducked his head. "I didn't go to college. No money. No time. But I read about this thing taking place at Harvard so I was going to try to sneak in."

She clapped. "So you got in and the rest is history?"

"No." Diego shook his head. "The attendees had these laminated passes and I didn't have one. They wouldn't let me in."

"Oh, I'm sorry."

"Best thing that ever happened to me."

"Why?"

"When I didn't get in, I went to this diner across the street. There was a group of the people who'd broken out of the lecture and I ended up meeting these guys and we…hit it off, and formed our own little club."

"What does your club do?"

"We ah, share business ideas, information, brainstorm through challenges, and generally support each other."

"That's…wonderful," she said softly. "It's so great that you have that support group."

"Yeah." Diego smiled. "They're an amazing bunch. And we've been there when each of us reaches milestones."

"So you see each other often?"

"Once a month we meet for breakfast." He laughed.

"That's really…great."

"I never would have the courage to approach them if I hadn't taken your words to heart."

"What words?"

"I figured out how to turn the failure into a success."

"My dad's words," she said bitterly. "Too bad he didn't follow his own advice, or maybe he did."

"I'm sorry about your parents." Even though he didn't necessarily have anything to apologize for, he continued. "I'm sorry London was being…difficult."

"That's a word for it." But Penny blinked.

"And I'm really sorry that I gave you a hard time. It wasn't fair of me." Something he prided himself on. He could see the hesitation in her eyes. He deliberately stepped forward into her personal space. "I unleashed my frustration with myself on you. Forgive me?"

"Yes."

LISA HUGHEY

Her breath caught. The lime green lace from her bra peeked out from beneath the thin tank top. Diego was fascinated with the smattering of freckles across her chest. He traced his fingers from one to the other, enthralled as her body vibrated beneath his light touch.

He followed the edge of the skimpy top until his fingers dipped into the valley between her breasts. Her heart thudded beneath his touch.

In complete accordance, they stood there. His breath a soft exhalation as he stared at his darker skin against her lighter skin.

Her hands were at his waist. She burrowed her fingers beneath his T-shirt, her nails scraped the taut skin of his stomach.

Diego leaned his forehead against hers, staring into her eyes as if he would find the answers to the universe.

In complete harmony, they breathed together.

His eyes drifted closed, committing this moment to memory. He bent his head, savoring the anticipation of their kiss. This intimacy somehow seemed more important, more profound, than the sex they'd had this morning.

The walkie-talkie squawked.

Penny jumped away from him.

"Crap. Sherry."

Tegan's voice confirmed Sherry had been found.

But the mood had been broken. "Got to go," Penny muttered.

Within seconds he was alone in the woods. She practically ran away and he had to wonder.

What just happened?

11

Diego couldn't sit still. He tapped his finger on his knee, studied Zinnia propped in her chair by the lake as she went on a fifteen-minute diatribe about being stuck here while everyone else had fun.

The campfire on the beach was in full swing.

Jeffrey London had bailed on the zipline and crafts session. Diego was pretty sure the guy was banging his assistant in his cabin, again. So Diego had done paperwork instead of playing. He had reviewed the contracts for the merger, making notes to discuss with his lawyer. He and London had dinner together but, after a brief smile and wave at the employees, the man had disappeared into his cabin again.

Their management styles were very different.

So now the music played and the employees sat around in small groups drinking beer and relaxing. The cohesion he'd hoped for wasn't happening. The clumps of people were clearly split along company lines. Diego treated his business like a family. He worked hard to keep a sense of community and camaraderie in place. Anyone on his staff could come to him with a suggestion or a problem. Yeah, it was true that in the last few years as they'd gotten even bigger that he'd grown farther and farther away from his company "family." But even so, the difference in corporate styles was patently obvious around the campfire.

London's employees were clearly restrained with Diego around. He'd retreated over to the Adirondack chairs away from the fire to keep Zin company, except she was driving him up the wall.

"I can't even drink," she grumbled.

He tried to tease her out of her mood. "Isn't that what got you in trouble in the first place?"

He scanned the crowd, searching for Penny. His mind kept wandering back to that moment right before she bolted.

He was confident enough to know when his interest was returned. And they had both been on the same page until that damn radio. But now she was avoiding him. He still might have been oblivious but during the casual cookout, she'd worked mostly behind the scenes. The few times he managed to catch her attention, her gaze had skittered away quickly.

He had no idea why.

Unfortunately Jeffrey London had continued to complain about Penny's program and the fact that she was here and that no way was he going to give a dime of London Automotive for some stupid program that had no benefit to his bottom line.

And all that complaining and anti-philanthropic spewing against Penny had put him in a foul mood.

"What's up your ass?" Zin turned on him.

Diego flushed. "Nothing."

"Nope. Not nothing. Give me something else to think about. I'm annoying myself."

Zin might be quite a few years younger but she had an old soul. More than once he'd confided in her when he'd been considering taking the business in a new direction.

Even so, no way was he explaining his current obsession with Penny. And his frustration that his upcoming business partner had a raging hard-on against her. "I'm puzzling out details and concerns about the merger."

Zin grimaced, her expression in the flickering firelight somewhat demonic.

"What?"

"Nothing."

"Now who's skipping out on the truth?"

"I know you want less work."

He wasn't afraid of hard work. "I used to work eighteen-hour days. I can handle a lot of work."

Zin nodded. "But that was different."

He hated to admit that she was right. He wanted different things than he'd wanted ten years ago. "My goal for forever has been to make it as an official member of the BBC."

Zin said softly, "Then merging is the right thing to do." But she bit her lip.

"You don't think I should do it?"

She stared into the flames.

"I had an interesting conversation with Penny earlier."

"The farmer girl?"

"Uh, yeah."

"You're awfully chummy with her." Zin's expression turned sly. "You like her?"

"I knew her before."

"Before?"

"We met years ago at camp."

"*This* camp?" Her delight was weirdly infectious. "Like when you were a kid?"

"Yeah." Diego clarified, "She was a camper when I was a counselor."

"Well, that's…a coincidence."

"Yeah. Got me thinking."

"About what?"

"About how sometimes your life can change in an instant."

"For good or for bad?"

"I'm…not sure." Diego continued to stew. He was caught between doing what was best for his business relationship with London and what he wanted to do with Penny.

He should just forget about this morning and move on.

But that didn't seem to be happening.

He couldn't stop thinking about her. And wanting her.

"Yeah, and we don't always realize how important something is until it's gone." Zinnia was uncharacteristically quiet.

Before he could ask what she was talking about, she distracted him.

"Hey, I forgot!" Zin dug into the small hobo bag tucked next to her hips. "I made you something."

"You made me something?"

"Friendship bracelets."

"Because they would go so well with my suits."

"I don't have to give it to you."

He'd hurt her feelings. Jesus, he was a dick. No wonder Penny had run away. "Thanks, Zin. *Lo siento.*" He knelt down beside her. "Tell me what you really think."

"You don't need me to tell you what you already know." Zin curled his fingers around the clunky wood bead bracelets. "I made two. In case you wanted to give one away. *Te amo.*"

"*También te amo.*" He kissed her cheek.

She pushed out of the chair awkwardly and hooked the crutches underneath her arms.

"My pain medicine kicked in." She looked around the camp. "I'm going to bed."

"You want me to walk you to your cabin?"

"It's hardly the inner city. I'll be fine." The circles beneath her eyes were more pronounced. She'd been a trooper through her broken ankle. "But I need you to stay until everyone is in their cabin for the night."

"Sure, Zin." Diego dropped into the chair by the lake and contemplated the fate of the world, or at least his own little slice of the world, in the flames.

PENNY COULDN'T WAIT to be done with this day.

She'd managed to stay out of Diego's sphere. She'd helped in the kitchen and delivered the industrial chafing dishes to the dining area. Then she'd worked to clear the

LISA HUGHEY

dining room after dinner all the while avoiding him. Tomorrow was going to be another long day.

Physically and emotionally she was spent. She'd been on edge all night.

But before she could crash, she had one last special delivery. Camp wouldn't be complete without s'mores around the fire.

The red Radio Flyer wagon with all-terrain wheels held boxes of Hershey bars, graham crackers and a huge bowl of marshmallows. Instead of metal coat hangers, the camp had long two-pronged stainless steel skewers. Fancy.

She tugged the wagon over to the picnic tables.

She'd be lying if she hadn't searched the shadows for Diego Ramos. The man haunted her past and now he was featured front and center in her all-grown-up daydreams.

Her X-rated daydreams, dammit.

And while they had definitely had a moment in the forest, the truth was his soon-to-be business partner hated her guts. No way was Diego going to get with her while Jeffrey London was in the picture.

She had enough abandonment issues. No need to add more.

Penny laid out the supplies for the treat on the cloth-covered tables. She set out the small metal waste can that reminded her of Oscar the Grouch's in *Sesame Street*. They had to make sure they cleaned up the food scraps, otherwise they'd end up with unwanted visitors to the campground.

The campers crowded around the table, laughing and joking and grabbing the marshmallows. Penny backed away from the chattering group and blended into the shadows.

Diego sat in one of the Adirondacks by the lake. While

everyone else laughed and danced and sang around the campfire, he was so very solitary. Very alone.

So different from that slightly scruffy kid he'd been. Now his shorts and T-shirt appeared to have been ironed. All buttoned up and neat, the only thing untidy about him right now was the beginnings of the beard on his jaw.

As if he'd started to allow a bit of that scruffy boy back in. But he wasn't quite ready to embrace that essence of his former self. Penny had the strangest urge to muss him up. To push him into allowing that kid back into his life.

Before she could rein in the impulse, she'd grabbed marshmallows and the metal campfire fork. She strode determinedly to the chair where he sat. He straightened. "Can I help you?"

"I'm here to help you." A bit of innuendo slipped into her voice, but hopefully he wouldn't notice.

She wasn't sure he'd play along.

"What if I said I don't need help?"

"I'd say you're wrong."

"What have you got?"

"Yummy goodness." She tossed a bag of marshmallows at him.

He caught the bag one-handed and turned it around to stare at the contents.

"No camp experience is complete without s'mores."

He was silent for another moment and she began to second-guess her impulsiveness.

Then he shot out of the chair. "You're right." He turned all that smoldering intensity on her.

He threaded marshmallows on the end of the fancy metal stick with a concentration that he showed in all things.

He'd been equally as intense when he'd pushed inside her this morning.

Her stomach fluttered at the memory.

He leaned into her. "What are you thinking about right now?"

Helplessly she stared back at him.

"Damn," he whispered.

They were at the edge of the campfire, more in the shadows than light. And her breath caught at the heated look in his eyes. She blindly shoved the marshmallows onto the stick.

She wanted him. Even more than she wanted to muss him up.

This was not her intention when she'd come over here. She had only wanted to alleviate his solitude. She needed to change the conversation before they did something they'd both regret.

They stood at the fire. Instead of looking at him, she fussed with the paper plates holding the graham cracker and chocolate bars. Desperate to alleviate the sexual tension, she shifted to his business pursuits.

"Your club have a name?"

DIEGO COULD HEAR the desperation in Penny's voice.

They were both on the edge of doing something they shouldn't. They needed to find neutral ground before he tossed his roasting marshmallow aside and they burned together.

"Yeah. It's um, silly." Except it wasn't. Every single one

of them had been striving to reach that pinnacle.

"I'm sure it's not."

"Billionaire Breakfast Club."

"Like the movie?"

"Yeah. With a few additions."

"You've got a nerd?"

Her eyes sparkled, and he had to shake off his lust and answer. "Peter Nguyen. Computer genius."

"A jock?"

"D'Andre Smith."

"The football player?"

So she knew her sports. Surprising. "Yep."

"You really know D'Andre?" She clasped his wrist, her fingers tight. "Can you get me an autograph?"

"Not a problem."

"Cool." She laughed. "A princess?"

"And a prince. Tracy Kennedy—but not the political family—and Jason Hollingsworth."

"The financier?"

"That's his father. Jay runs a Venture Capitalist firm, JayCo."

Penny. "A misfit?"

"Duke, he's a surfer and a community activist, and Courtney, she's a gamer girl."

"Wait, I think I've heard of her. She got doxxed and now she's running for Congress."

He was so fucking proud of her refusal to back down in the face of the trolls who'd harassed her. "Yep."

"A rebel?"

"That's me."

"And you're all billionaires?" Her eyebrows rose.

"Not yet." This deal with London would clinch it. Except he was standing here with her, thinking things he shouldn't, and Jeffrey London and his inconvenient and totally irrational hatred of Penny was definitely an obstacle to Diego's goals. The dude was cock-blocking him and didn't even know it.

"That's really impressive."

Diego shrugged. "Some of it was luck."

"Luck you made," she corrected.

He was pretty damn lucky, he thought as he stared into her shadowed green eyes. She bit her lip and looked away at the fire.

"Meeting you was lucky," he said. "Now, and back then." Why not lay it on the line?

"Now is just a camp crush." Penny shook her head. "It's the atmosphere and the fact that you're outside your everyday activities. Like a vacation romance."

Crush? He wanted to argue.

Before he could, she turned and shoved her marshmallow into the flames.

Everyone else had already gorged on the sugary treat. Beyond the flames, the clunk of metal cans tossed into the recycling bin and the murmur of multiple conversations formed background noise.

Once the marshmallow was charred she grabbed the crackers and clumsily squeezed it between them. The chocolate melted, running down the side of her hand.

Penny took a bite, and more chocolate ran over her fingers. "Mmm. So good." She reached for a napkin. But Diego had a better idea.

✿ 12 ✿

Diego lifted Penny's hand to his mouth and licked the chocolate. "Don't want any to go to waste." His rough fingers circled her wrist, holding her in place. His tongue lapped at her skin and tingles spread from her fingertips throughout her body.

"What—" her throat suddenly tight. What was he doing? "—was that for?"

He pulled away and grinned. "Don't want you to get dirty."

A smear of chocolate clung to his upper lip. Without thinking she leaned in and sucked the sweet from his mouth.

The moment was fraught with an odd tension. The crackle of the fire, the scent of wood smoke filled her senses, and yet she could still smell the essence of him.

Amusement sparkled in his chocolate eyes, even more rich and sinful than the candy he'd just licked from her flesh.

"Nothing wrong with a little dirty," Penny said huskily.

"Not at all." He sobered, the shadows in his dark eyes

hovered, and she couldn't stand to see that playful spirit dimmed. Her attention shifted to what was left of her s'more. The marshmallow was in danger of falling to the ground.

"In my opinion, dirty is underrated." And then she scooped that bit of melted marshmallow onto her thumb and painted his mouth.

"You're going there?" His face darkened. Maybe she'd pushed it too far. He licked some of the marshmallow off his lips and then smiled. It was a wicked smile, promising retribution.

"In for a penny, in for a pound." She took the last bite of her s'more and smashed it against his mouth. Waited to see what he'd do.

His smile brightened, intensified. Then he laughed, the rich low rumble seemed to surprise him.

"You went there." He laughed again and suddenly she knew what he was going to do next.

Run! She needed to run. But she couldn't run because she had to stay until the last camper was in for the night.

But she couldn't help it. She took a step back. It wasn't a retreat exactly. Okay, it was a retreat.

DIEGO BLINKED at Penny's audacity.

She had just smashed s'mores in his face.

No one he knew would dare mess him up the way she had just done. The need to retaliate welled up inside him. "You're going to pay for that," he growled.

He loaded his finger with melted chocolate and pressed it against her mouth.

Her lips parted in a laugh. Her tongue peeked between the plump unpainted lips, but before she could lick it off, he painted a trail over her chin and along her neck. He lingered in the hollow of her throat.

Her pulse thudded beneath his fingertips. No longer laughing, she swallowed, the muscles in her neck clenching then releasing.

"I can't fucking wait to lick this off you." He continued painting her skin with the chocolate, down the middle of her chest until he dipped his finger into the valley between her breasts. She quivered beneath the sensual caress.

Diego glanced around the campfire, making sure they were hidden in the shadows. Whatever this was, he wasn't about to expose her to the censure from London's employees. But while he and Penny had been roasting marshmallows and playing paint the numbers, the rest of the party had cleared out.

He and Penny were alone in the dark night. Only the crackle of the fire and the buzz of insects surrounded them now. He tugged her over to the Adirondack chair he'd abandoned earlier and pulled her into his lap. He bent her back over his arm. Her silky hair tumbled over his biceps and he wanted to bury his fist in the mass and tug her so he could feast on her neck.

Diego snapped open the front hook to her bra.

He buried his nose between her breasts, nuzzling the small mounds with his beard and licking the chocolate from her skin.

With everyone gone, he pushed her top down, exposing

her to the firelight and his avid gaze. He cupped her in his palm and pushed her into his mouth. Rolling the tight bud, he tongued her hard.

She arched into the intimate kiss.

Penny's nails scraped the base of his neck, scattering goose bumps across his skin. His cock hardened in a rush.

Her face flushed and her eyes half closed, she clutched his head between her hands and moaned.

In a frantic move, she burrowed beneath his tight T-shirt and ripped the cotton over his head. She explored his chest, running her fingers through the smattering of hair and over the muscles in his shoulders, her strong hands smoothed over his biceps and along his forearms. She rolled into his embrace and began to kiss his skin. Her teeth nipped gently at his nipples.

His cock beat against the curve of her ass.

Fuck me. If he didn't shift her away from his lower body, he was going to come in his shorts.

The slightly illicit location out in the open, where anyone could come back to the fire, fueled the passion between them. For years, he'd done everything right. Weighed every word, every action. But in this moment, he threw it all away. He wanted her now.

Her nipples glistened from his attention. He unbuttoned her shorts, spread his fingers along her belly. She contracted at the light touch, and when he slid his fingers into her curls and fingered the swollen bud, she shuddered in his arms.

"We should stop," he murmured against her skin. Giving her an out if she needed it.

But he couldn't seem to stop playing with her clit.

Penny shook her head. "No, we shouldn't."

He was thinking about her. About the fact that she was half naked, his hands down her pants. "You're in a compromising position right now."

She bit his collarbone. "Well then, let's compromise you too."

He couldn't believe how much he loved that idea. "Hell, yes."

She sucked a kiss against the sensitive spot below his ear.

He pinched her nipple in response.

Penny wrestled with the button to his country club shorts. Then she ripped the zipper down and dug into his briefs. With a smooth move, she'd curled her work-roughened hands around his cock.

Fuck.

Penny lifted from his lap. He grabbed for her, but she was only changing positions. She straddled his lap and fisted his cock. Her breasts, tumbling from the hem of her top, gleamed in the moonlight. Her face was flushed with desire, her lips puffy with the force of their kisses.

"I want inside you." But they didn't have a condom.

Sadly he didn't think there were any orgasm donor packets lying around. "Protection?" He asked hopefully.

She bit her lip and shook her head.

"We'll have to improvise." *Damn. I have to get inside her any way I can.* "I'm going to fuck you with my fingers then."

Penny nodded.

Her eyelids drooped and her head tilted back. Moonlight limning her features, like a moon goddess, she tilted her head and let the light rain over her.

In one quick move, he slid his fingers inside her sex. He rubbed her G-spot, caressing the inflamed knot into a higher state of arousal. She was slick against his fingers, and her hips rocked in time to his stroke. Her hand moved up and down his cock, tightening every time he coaxed another low moan from her. Together they found an erotic rhythm.

She was straddling him, her tanned and strong legs lifted up and down to the rhythm of his thrusts. Her knees braced next to his legs as her soft ass rubbed against his hairy thighs.

She was so wet. She dripped on his hand.

They moved in a crazy rhythm, reaching for each other, oblivious to the surroundings.

When was the last time he'd even engaged in this kind of play? Ever since his twentieth birthday he'd been focused on making the business successful. He'd lost the simple pleasures of connection and lust. Every person in his life was chosen for maximum benefit. And if they couldn't do something for him, then they weren't worth the effort.

Diego had to keep his eye on the endgame.

The prize.

But not tonight.

Tonight, she was his reward, his prize.

Like a proper victor, he was going to claim her.

PENNY WAS HAVING AN OUT-OF-BODY MOMENT.

Her clothes were disheveled, and her breasts bounced in the moonlight as she rode Diego's fingers. His cock was thick and long and close to erupting in her hand.

She had never in her life thrown caution away and given in to her sexual desires. The fact that they were out in the woods, around the campfire where anyone could see them should have stopped her cold.

Instead the forbidden location titillated her. Aroused her. Did that make her wrong? She didn't know. But as Diego's pre-come slicked her hand, she knew he was close and she decided she could worry about existential crises later.

He conquered her body with two fingers and his mouth nearly sent her over the edge. But she didn't want to go alone. Was determined to make this ultra-controlled man lose his tight grip before she did.

She was holding her orgasm at bay tenuously, as she rolled her fist over the head of his cock. Goddamn, had he gotten bigger? He seemed to swell in her hand, and she wished again that she'd thought to tuck a condom in her shorts pocket.

Then Diego twisted his fingers, lurched up and sucked her nipple into his mouth. That little bite of pain pushed her over the edge. Her body convulsed around his fingers as her orgasm rose over her in a crazy swell and took her under. Fireworks burst through her in a cascade of light and heat.

Her long, low moan was drowned out by his groan.

Hot jets of liquid splashed against her stomach as he let go of his control.

Diego pressed his thumb against her clit, and another set of quakes shimmied through her body. She continued to pump his erection until he had nothing more to give, then she collapsed against his chest.

Penny draped her body over Diego, limp, replete, completely wrung out.

What was it about him that made her abandon all sense of the right thing to do and just…toss aside her inhibitions?

They were out in the middle of the woods for fuck's sake.

Technically she was working. She buried her head in his neck. "Can't believe we did that."

His body was warm and tense beneath her. They were both sticky from the combination of s'mores and sex. He lazily licked a spot of chocolate from her jaw. "Yum."

"How do you convince me to just throw all sense out the window?"

"It's a gift."

She chuckled against his neck, then kissed that spot beneath his ear that caused him to shiver. He tasted of man and sweat and salt. His hairy legs tickled the sensitive backs of her thighs.

And impossibly she began to tingle again. He was joking, and yet his words were true.

He was the gift.

Maybe a small one and she'd have to return it and forget about him after this weekend. But right this moment, she felt too satisfied to worry about it.

She'd just accept it for now and deal with the aftermath later.

13

Diego had done a lot of stupid in his life but having sex with Penny out in the open last night was beyond crazy. She tempted him. And worse, it hadn't felt stupid.

But as his watch beeped, he knew he needed to get going.

He rolled away from her naked body. They were in his cabin. It had been closer than hers. They'd hastily cleaned up the campfire, and doused the embers of the fire, before stoking their own sexual fire again.

He showered and dressed quickly, putting on his suit and a clean shirt and tie.

He was late as it was. The Billionaire Breakfast Club was going to be annoyed with him. But as he looked back at the wood nymph lying in his bed, he couldn't be sorry.

He closed the door on last night and headed back to Boston.

He had been planning to miss this month's get-together because of the retreat, but D'Andre had set up an interview

LISA HUGHEY

to plug the next iteration of his safety helmet, and the magazine wanted a photo op of all seven of them. So Zin had found a heliport nearby. He planned to buzz into Boston for breakfast and the interview, and be back at the camp after lunch.

Diego rubbed his cleanly shaved jaw. After two days of scruff, his smooth skin felt weird, like he didn't quite fit in that image anymore.

He strode into the diner. All the guys were already here. They were an unlikely bunch. D'Andre Smith, former North Carolina linebacker, former pro-football player, and now CEO of his own company.

Jason Hollingsworth the Fourth—Jay—always looked like he was headed out for cocktails, even at nine a.m. on a Sunday. Except he'd become Diego's partner and friend. Who would have ever thought a second-generation Puerto Rican guy from Dot and a guy whose family came to America on the *Mayflower* and practically created the social register would be besties?

Peter Nguyen was their resident nerd, except these days he worked out and that skinny, socially awkward kid he'd met fourteen years ago was gone. Peter had been the first to hit billionaire status.

Duke, surfer dude and social activist, still looked like he spent his nights sleeping on the beach and his days surfing. His blond hair was on the edge of stringy and his face tanned and healthy.

The girls weren't here yet.

"Nice of you to make it." D'Andre mock jabbed at him.

"I was in the Berkshires," he said mildly. He was trying to hold onto that relaxed, sated happy from last night so he

138

refused to fight with the guy. D wasn't really even mad. He just had an excess of aggression since he'd retired from the NFL last year.

Jay lifted a blond brow. "Someone got laid."

"Hey, that's great." Peter Nguyen, his face broke into a huge smile. "Me too!"

"Jesus, Nguyen. TMI." Duke shook his head.

"Didn't you have your high school reunion last night?" D'Andre and Peter had become fast friends. The kid who barely passed and the kid with a perfect SAT score had bonded immediately over the curse of high school stereotypes.

"Yes." Pete flushed.

D'Andre high-fived Pete.

Tracy, princess of high society and Jay's childhood friend, and Courtney, their resident gamer girl—another unlikely friendship—burst into the diner, arm in arm.

Courtney's hardware was prominently displayed, and she was totally gothed out.

Jay frowned at her. "Is that appropriate interview attire?"

Courtney stuck out her pierced tongue at him and shot back, "Is that a silver spoon up your butt?"

Diego sighed. Jay and Courtney were the only ones who barely tolerated each other. Weirdly, their little band of misfits had become just what Peter Nguyen had predicted all those years ago. After they'd escaped from the Harvard Young Entrepreneurs symposium and Diego had crashed their impromptu meetup, they'd traded ideas and talked business strategy for hours. Everyone in the odd group had shared what they wanted to accomplish and what they thought they needed to do to get there.

Just like in *The Breakfast Club* movie, they had formed a strange connection.

Except their pact had not only survived, but thrived. They'd been there for each other's successes and the failures, continuing to encourage each other through both the good and the bad.

The BBC had ended up being his sounding board. They consulted each other. It helped that none of their businesses overlapped. But they'd never steered him wrong.

"What's wrong?" Tracy asked.

"What do you mean?" Nothing was wrong. Except he'd had the short helicopter ride to think about last night. And what he'd figured out was he didn't want to give Penny up.

But there was more at stake than just him.

"C'mon. It's corporate retreat weekend, right?"

"Yes."

"How's it going?"

Diego considered the weekend but business had taken a back seat to Penny. She was all he could think about. "I reviewed the numbers on Thursday and they look good."

Tracy put her hand on his forearm. "Numbers aren't the only component to a successful merger."

Easy for her to say. Her social media company was going IPO next month, and the preliminary scuttlebutt was they were going to blow it out of the water.

"Does this have anything to do with the woman?" D'Andre prodded, finding another way to jab at Diego.

Like a predator scenting weakness Tracy narrowed in for the kill. "Woman? What woman?"

One drunken weekend years ago, he'd shared his original story with the breakfast club. How that moment in the parking lot with Penny had changed him. They all had their own versions of "Turn that failure into a success" but his had been the most dramatic. Except possibly for Jay's.

"It was her." Diego had so many conflicting emotions from that memory. Except now Penny was all grown up and that long-ago remorse had been replaced by an inconvenient lust.

Tracy jerked back. "The little girl? The one who pretty much started your obsession with success?"

"Obsession." Diego laughed. "That's a little harsh."

Except no one else was laughing.

Diego glanced around the table. He was the odd man out. He was the only one of them who didn't go to college, even though D'Andre had only gone one year before going into the draft and Jay had dropped out as a giant fuck-you to his father. Diego was the only one who had never even considered it. But he had street knowledge.

"Let's face it," Peter said. "You've always felt like you had more to prove than the rest of us."

Diego blinked, stunned. He couldn't wrap his brain around what they were saying.

"Yeah, man." D'Andre shook his head. "You took that damn name so literally."

Billionaire Breakfast Club.

"Yeah, we're all going to make it." Courtney tugged on her cartilage ring. "Or some version of it, but—"

"Money isn't everything," Jay interrupted her.

She shot him an annoyed frown.

"Easy for you to say, you've always had it." Now he was starting to get a little fucking defensive.

"Dude, it's mostly just a way to keep score," Duke said.

"Or do something good with. No one person can use that much money," Pete continued.

But Diego was spinning, feeling lost like when Jay had convinced him to go sailing. He was a "feet firmly on the ground" kind of guy, and didn't mind boating on a lake, but when they'd been bouncing on the waves with the shore barely in sight, the ocean had felt too vast.

Now he was floundering as his world view shifted.

Jay nudged him. "So what happened?"

What had happened? And why couldn't he clear out the noise?

"Let's get back to the personal." Tracy rubbed her hands together like an evil genius about to wreak havoc on the world.

"Tell us more about this chick." Of all of them Courtney was the most protective. For all her tough exterior, she had a marshmallow center.

"Maybe he doesn't want to talk about the personal," Jason said, coming to his rescue.

Except maybe he did want to share.

"We, ah," Diego hesitated.

"Wait this is like, romantic?" Tracy grabbed his hand and clutched his fingers in hers. "Oh my gosh!"

"They had sex. That doesn't necessarily translate to romantic." Jay flattened his palms on the Formica tabletop.

"We all know your views on that," Courtney said flatly.

Some tension simmered between Jay and Courtney. Worse than usual. Diego wondered what was up with them.

"So, what next?" Duke leaned back into the booth, his arms crossed.

"I don't know. She's amazing." Diego couldn't help but smile. She made him happy. "But there's a history with Jeffrey London."

"Oh, ugh," Tracy made a horrified face. "Jerky Jeffrey, the creeper? Every single woman at the country club stays far away from him."

D'Andre asked, "She works for him?"

"No. She's a farmer."

"A farmer?"

"Right? And she's at the camp this weekend pitching her new non-profit. She's trying to convince companies to plant small gardens for employees to work in as stress relief."

D'Andre perked up.

Diego recited a quick overview of Penny's idea.

Duke said, "I'm in love with this girl already."

"That's…a brilliant idea." Jay cocked his head to the side clearly thinking about Penny's mission.

"Yeah." He thought about this weekend. His mouth curved into a smile. Could he attribute his calm and reduced stress from being in nature and working with the garden project? Or was Penny the better influence?

"You really like her."

"Maybe I just like the idea." He wasn't sure how he felt about Penny. All he knew was the depth of feeling was too new, too tenuous, too crazy. Too impulsive. He didn't do impulsive. "But London hates her."

"So, London Automotive isn't working out?" Jay asked.

"On paper, it looks great." Diego finally acknowledged that while the general business merger made sense, he and

London were radically different in their management styles.

Jay was nodding. "If you recall, I was hesitant to broker the original meet."

"Yeah." Diego had ignored his friend's reservations because he'd really wanted to take Ramos Classic Auto Restoration to the next level.

"Oh goody." Courtney tapped her fingers on the tabletop, her rings clinking. "Let's strategize."

Diego needed to focus on business but he didn't really need strategizing. They'd already done that. "About the merger?"

"You've totally already made up your mind." Tracy let go of his hand.

She was right. He had.

Diego blinked. He had. Wow. "Then what are we strategizing about?"

"About the girl." Courtney grinned, her lip ring catching the light.

"But...she isn't business."

"The BBC is past that." Tracy was always the romantic. "This is more important. It's life."

❧ 14 ❧

Diego wasn't at the presentation this morning.

Inside she was withering.

But she'd be damned if she let anyone know it. She learned early to smile and persevere through pain and humiliation when her parents skipped town. She could handle one more day of pretending all was well and that his snub hadn't hurt her.

Penny smiled and joked through her presentation, advising the campers on how to properly plant the small seedlings and espousing the benefits of getting out in nature and working with dirt.

And she concealed her hurt.

She'd woken to an empty bed and the click of the door. Diego was gone.

He'd left.

Just...left.

She was tired, sore, and embarrassed that she'd fallen for

someone who didn't really give a shit. He'd rather bolt from his own cabin than wake up to her. That was rough.

A serious blow to her ego. But even more to her heart.

Even better, Jeffrey London was in attendance this morning. After blowing off most of the retreat, the big boss had put in an appearance.

He'd scowled at her through her entire presentation.

"What's in this for you?" he sneered, asking in front of everyone.

Her fee was nominal, covering the costs of the nonprofit. Any extra dollar she could pour back into the project was a win for expanding the program beyond Boston. "The project will benefit both the companies and their communities."

"And you think people should trust *you* with their money?" He barked out a laugh. He was trying to publicly humiliate her. She got that. But she wasn't her parents.

"I'm working on getting donations from gardening supply companies to reduce the cost to the companies." She smiled at Alma, who looked thrilled.

Except Alma's boss was nowhere to be found. And his absence was like a flashing beacon that he didn't support the program.

"My counterpart didn't even bother to attend this…presentation."

Fuck him. "Mr. Ramos was here a day early and I was able to explain the program to him in detail then. Perhaps he had some business to attend to."

"Like we'd trust our business to you." London continued to cut her down. "Look at you."

Sure, Penny wasn't really dressed in business attire, but come on, they were in the middle of the freaking woods.

"Thanks, everyone. If you want more information, the details of the program will be available online at my farm website, www dot Pretty Penny Farms dot com slash Agriphilanthropy." She smiled even though her heart hurt. "Remember to have me initial your bingo cards."

The campers stuck around, asking questions. Diego's employees really seemed to be on board with the idea. She signed a lot of cards and chatted with people as Penny packed up the trowels and small shovels and gloves into a cardboard box.

Finally Alma was the last to leave. Penny heaved the box into her arms and headed for her pickup truck. She also still had the Charger here. So she was going to have to get someone to drive the truck home later tonight or tomorrow morning since both her vehicles were here.

Her first instinct was to get the hell out of camp. But she couldn't just leave. She'd promised to stay through the rest of the camp. In exchange, Michael and Heather Tully agreed to put a lead box to her website on the Camp Firefly Falls website.

She paused for a moment and surveyed the newly planted raised beds. A fierce satisfaction buzzed inside her. She'd had this dream for a while and now the farm was doing well enough for her to channel some of her energy toward this project.

She wasn't going to let Jeffrey London and Diego Ramos derail her. She was stronger than that.

She lugged the box out to the employee parking lot,

studiously avoiding the Porsche at the end of the lot. So he was here. Jerk. He could have at least shown up for her presentation.

Whatever.

Penny pulled down the gate on the bed of the truck and hefted the box in. She turned to go back for the rest of her supplies but Jeffrey London was unnervingly close. She hadn't heard him follow her.

He loomed over her. "Do you really think you're going to get away with this?"

Get away with this? "Excuse me?"

"No way am I going to allow you to swindle people and companies out of their hard-earned money."

Penny flashed back to the last time she'd had a confrontation in this parking lot.

Diego's angry teenage face as he opened her world to the realities of people who didn't have her life.

"My goal is to create gardens to help feed people." Penny's temper simmered but she held back. Maybe Jeffrey London didn't realize that plenty of people go hungry at night. "People, kids go to bed hungry all the time."

Be polite. Be polite. She chanted in her head. She couldn't afford to piss off the London Automotive CEO for multiple reasons. First and foremost, she needed good word of mouth, not bad press.

"Right." He sneered at her again. "You think once people find out about your parents they're going to invest with you?"

"This is about doing something good and paying it forward."

"After you pay yourself, right?"

Penny had had enough. "This is a nonprofit venture. If you listened to my presentation—"

"Like anyone will believe a Hastings."

"My family name is hardly—"

"No one is going to support you." London spit out the words. He clenched his fist and his face turned bright red. "Not if I have anything to say about it."

Why did he hate her so much? This couldn't be about her, could it? "What do you have against helping people in need?"

"You keep peddling that. But I know better. I'll make it my personal mission to destroy you."

"Are you threatening me?"

"You think I don't recognize a con when I see it," London said. "Everyone is out for themselves."

"FEED Together isn't a con, it's a 501c nonprofit organization."

"Bullshit."

Penny's heart pounded as his animosity battered at her. So filled with hate. And lack of compassion for others. "I'm sorry you feel that way. But my goal is to feed people using corporate sponsorship."

"I'll bet you want to be sponsored." London's gaze was fixed behind Penny. "You keep trying to sell this, I'll pull my agreement to the merger."

Penny frowned. "I have nothing to do with your business with Diego Ramos." But if he threatened Diego's business, she would have to back off. She'd never take his dream away from him.

A rustling behind her was her only warning. She turned around and Diego was there.

Penny had been so focused on Jeffrey London she hadn't even realized that Diego had been there all the time. He stood between his open car door and the body of the Porsche, watching and listening to the exchange between her and London.

"Ramos might have fallen for your bullshit. But once I'm in charge, there's no way we'll move forward."

With that he stopped her cold.

While she wanted to tell him where to go, she wouldn't do anything to negatively impact Diego's future. She understood how long he'd been working toward his goal. Even if he was a dick.

She didn't look at Diego. He'd already rejected her once today. Her humiliation factor was pretty much at two hundred percent right now.

But in that moment, she wanted him to stick up for her. To defend her to London.

His absolute silence said it all.

Devastation hollowed her out. But her heart was still there. Still beat in her chest, the thud echoed in her ears.

Penny lifted her chin, narrowed her gaze. "You are a horrible human being."

No one said anything.

"If you'll excuse me." Penny tilted up her chin and swept out of the parking lot, holding on to her anger and her frustration. But as soon as she was out of sight of the parking lot, she began to tremble with a combination of rage and sickness and a crushing sense of hurt.

She'd been abandoned once again.

❧

DIEGO WATCHED PENNY GO. Her back straight, shoulders stiff.

He'd seen the moment she'd given up defending herself. As soon as Jeffrey London threatened Diego, she stopped pushing the asshat.

He'd been trying to give her room to defend herself. But he thought maybe he'd fucked up. The look on her face....

He needed to go after her. But first, he had one last piece of business.

Diego stalked toward London. "What was that about?"

"There's no way I'm giving that girl a penny," London said. His animosity burned in his eyes.

Diego asked, "What do you have against her?"

"Her family are cheaters. Liars. The worse scum around. Her parent's stole over a hundred thousand dollars from my mother. She paid in advance for furnishings, decorations and they skipped the country with her money." A trail of spittle edged out the corner of his mouth. "My mother was humiliated, not to mention the financial loss."

Diego studied him. "You shouldn't judge her for her parent's sins."

Jeffrey London's lip curled. "She's no innocent."

Huh. He was tired of weighing every word he spoke. Tired of the sheer mental energy expended by saying the right thing, the right way, to the right people. "You have a wife."

"What does that have to do with anything?"

Did he not see the hypocrisy? "You're—" *banging*, "—sleeping with your assistant." Maybe Diego wasn't quite ready to completely throw out his penchant for political correctness.

"And?" His face reddened. "That's hardly your business."

"True. But it makes you a cheater," Diego said.

"What?" London hissed, his face turning an unhealthy shade of red.

"I like the program."

"Forget it." London slashed his hand down. "No way is our company going to give her a dime."

"You're right about one thing."

"What's that?"

"*Our* company won't give her any money."

A rustling on the path startled him. Fuck. Penny was quickly heading back toward the lodge. He had been so intent on Jeffrey London he hadn't noticed she'd returned.

London smirked. Why had Diego never noticed that smarmy edge to him? "I'm glad you see it my way."

Diego wanted to run after Penny. But he needed to take care of this first. "Nope. There isn't going to be an *our* company."

"What the hell are you talking about?" London sputtered.

"I've decided not to proceed with the merger."

"You aren't serious."

"As a heart attack." Diego smiled. A huge weight lifted from him. His body already felt lighter, freer, happier. Holy shit, did this feel good.

"But—but, you need me." London wasn't smirking any more. "You need me far more than I need you."

"That might be true if I expanded. But turns out I don't need to expand to get what I want."

London couldn't seem to wrap his head around what Diego meant. "What do you want?"

"The girl."

15

"You've got to be kidding." London's face was full of outrage. "You can't do this to me. To your business."

But he was wrong. Diego could and would. Happiness lit him up from the inside. The same joy he felt in Penny's presence. Except based on the way she'd hustled away, she clearly didn't think he would stand up for her.

"Nope. Not kidding. And yep, I sure can."

"You're going to let that piece of trash—"

Bam. Diego's fist hit London's jaw before he even registered he was going to swing.

The older man rocked back. His eyes wild, his face already swelling. "You aren't going to get away with this. I'll sue."

"I'll be sure to send all the details to your lawyer, and your wife." Fuck it. London wanted to play hardball, Diego would play.

That shut the guy up.

Damn, that punch felt good. Diego shook out his hand,

rubbing his knuckles. "Don't fuck with me." He leaned against the trunk of Penny's Charger and waited for the guy to leave.

"You're going to be sorry." London stomped off.

His first instinct was to run after Penny. Fall at her feet and grovel. But as he calmed his racing heartbeat, he knew he needed a solid plan. He'd failed just now, but no way would he just give up. But he had to come up with a way to turn this into a success.

❧

STUPID. She'd been stupid to linger in the shadows hoping that Diego would stick up for her. Penny raced back toward the lodge.

Diego's words echoing in her head. *You're right about one thing.* Our *company won't give her any money.*

She was a total fool. When Jeffrey London threatened Diego, she'd immediately backed off to save him. To save his business deal.

And what had he done? Agreed with that asshole London.

She was gutted. Like someone had taken a plastic spoon and scooped out her insides. A big gaping hole opened inside her and threatened to swallow her. She rubbed her breastbone, trying to massage away the ache.

Stupid. Stupid. Stupid.

She needed to close off, shut down, and not give London or Diego the satisfaction of knowing how much they had hurt her.

Penny's steps slowed, and she trudged toward the lodge,

thinking about how much could change in such a short time. She'd been so happy. So thrilled to be back here.

So hopeful for the future.

The farm was doing well. She was finally about to launch her dream project. She had her life together.

And then for a short bit, she let Diego Ramos derail her. Screw that.

She refused to let Jeffrey London and Diego Ramos scuttle her plans. Every step away from him, her hurt diminished and her anger grew. By the time Penny got to the lodge she was fuming.

No man was going to ruin her dreams. He was the one missing out. He was the one who left. But she was a survivor. She'd survive this. And somehow, some way, she'd turn the failure into a success.

❧

"ZIN." Diego jogged toward his cousin. She was on an Adirondack chair, out by the lake, watching the rest of the CAR employees swim in the sparkling water.

For a second, his brain stuttered. Penny had rocked his world on that chair. And he was damned if he'd let that go.

"Why are you still dressed for your interview?"

He glanced down at his suit and muddy shoes. "I need you."

Zin frowned at him. "I just saw Penny. She didn't look very happy."

"I fucked up."

"Typical."

"I need your help," he said impatiently.

"By all means, let me drop everything."

"Please." He didn't have time to argue with her. "It's for Penny."

"Well since you asked so nicely."

"Zin."

"What are you planning?"

"I have part of it down. I want to fix her car," Diego said.

"That's romantic." The eye roll was exaggerated. And if she could reach him he was pretty sure she'd have hit him upside the head.

"C'mon Zin. I need the parts. Can you take care of it?"

"That's not going to be near enough to fix how upset she was."

"I know."

"So what else you got?"

"I'm working on it." But his stomach rolled. It needed to be *epic* so there would be no question he chose her. Diego thought over what she'd shared with him.

"I hurt her."

"How?"

"London criticized her, said something, and I didn't immediately jump in."

"Yeah. He was pretty harsh during her presentation this morning."

Shit. "Fuck him." Diego wanted to punch Jeffrey London all over again.

Zin shoved upright, finally really paying attention. "What about merging?"

"I'll find another way." Or maybe he wouldn't. Maybe he and his company were just fine where they were at.

"Oh, thank God." The relief on her face made him pause.

"Really?" Diego drew back from her. "What about the money we would have made?"

"You were the one who was so set on more money." She brushed her palm against his cheek. "When is more than plenty too much?"

According to his friends, the billionaire part of the breakfast club was really just more of a guideline. His worldview had shifted at that realization. He'd been so focused on the end result he hadn't been paying attention to the present. Always striving for that elusive number, he hadn't taken the time to appreciate right now.

"I need to focus on what's important."

"Let's get started then."

"I may have wrecked it."

Zin teased, "It'll buff right out."

Great. That's what he said when a car was a total loss.

"I was looking for encouragement, Zin." Had he blown his chance? Only one way to find out.

❧ 16 ❧

One hour later and Zin had gotten him the parts. Special delivery. He'd have to give her a raise.

So here he was, in the employee parking lot of Camp Firefly Falls, getting a wrench on Penny's Charger and implementing his plan to show her how special she was.

The smell of engine grease combined with the scent of blooming pink bushes flooded his senses. He was urgently tinkering, thinking about how happy she would be when she found out what he'd done. Maybe she'd forgive him by showing her gratitude in a physical way.

"What are you doing?" Penny cried.

Diego jumped, banged his head on the open hood.

"Ow." Shit. He'd been so lost in his fantasy of Penny showing her appreciation, he hadn't heard her approach.

He rubbed the bump on the back of his head, smiled at her. "I wanted to apologize."

"By sabotaging my car?"

What? "No, no. I'm *fixing* your problem." He had grease

on his fingers, so he didn't want to get her dirty. Yet he was hyperconscious of the need to grab hold of her so she couldn't run away.

"I'm perfectly capable of getting my own car fixed." Penny crossed her arms defensively. She was dressed in her jeans shorts and a tank top with "Get My Dirt On" in script across her lovely breasts. "My local garage just shut down and I haven't had a chance to find someone who works on old cars."

"Classic. It's not *old*, it's classic." Diego gripped his wrench, and asked what he'd been considering since he realized she drove a Charger. "Why this car?"

Because, it had occurred to him that this specific car was common, but not that common.

She flushed. "I liked the way it looked."

"I used to have this exact model."

"Is that so?" Penny said casually. "I guess you traded it for that crazy expensive impractical sports car."

"Nope. I had to sell my Charger." Diego grabbed a rag from the toolbox at his feet and rubbed the grease off his fingers. For a moment, he paused. The scent of engine grease, and motor oil, and lubricant swirled around him like a welcome memory. He patted her engine and remembered all the hours he'd spent getting his first car just right.

God, he'd loved that car. It had seen him through the first years of trying to find his way in business and given him the kernel of the idea that became Ramos Classic Auto Restoration.

A wide smile spread over his face.

She'd edged closer, peered under the hood of the car. "You seem awfully happy about having to sell your car."

"Nope. It killed me to sell her."

"But?"

"But the profits provided the seed money for Ramos Classic Auto Restoration."

"That's what you do?" She tried to disguise her interest. "Supply parts for classic cars?"

"That's what we started out doing. A sort of eBay for classic auto parts."

"Well, that still doesn't explain why you're working on my car."

"I told you." Diego eased the hood down gently, then patted the blue paint. "To apologize."

"Most people just say 'I'm sorry.'"

"I'm not most people."

"Well, congrats to you."

Was it wrong that the snotty tone kind of turned him on? Diego took a step toward her.

She stepped back, those gorgeous green eyes narrowed in suspicion. "What are you doing now?"

"Trying to get closer to you."

"I don't want you to get closer." But her mouth trembled, and Penny bounced on her tiptoes as if she was getting ready to bolt.

"Don't go."

"Why?"

"Because you haven't accepted my apology."

"Fine. I accept. Bye." She started to leave.

Dammit. He knew it couldn't be easy.

Diego grabbed her wrist, stopped her. The bones beneath his fingers were delicate, feminine. "Penny."

"What?" She faced toward the lodge, not looking at him. And the happiness he'd felt shimmered away.

He rubbed his thumb on her wrist. Saw her shiver. "I'm sorry."

"What are you sorry about?" She still hadn't turned around.

Diego held on to her wrist. She wasn't moving, neither away or turning toward him. At this point, he'd consider that a victory. "You didn't stay to hear what London and I agreed upon," he said softly.

"So formal," she mocked. "And I heard you. 'Our company won't give her any money.'"

"That's because there isn't going to be an *our* company."

She whirled around breaking his light hold. "What?"

"I called off the merger."

"But…I thought you needed it to achieve your goals." Her eyes were wide, uncertain.

"My goals changed."

"But—"

"I had to go to Boston this morning. The breakfast club had an interview."

She blinked. "And you're already back?"

"Helicopters are wicked efficient for short range travel."

"I thought you'd left." That soft hurt in her voice killed him.

"Not a chance."

She hadn't bolted away from him. She also hadn't thrown herself into his arms and shown her undying gratitude.

Diego had to ramp it up. "I wasn't happy."

"That's too bad."

"I realized after talking to my friends that getting to billionaire status wasn't what I needed."

Penny stiffened, stared over his shoulder at what he was sure was a fascinating tree.

Diego curled a finger under her chin, lifted her head so she could meet his gaze. "Don't you want to know what I need?"

"None of my business." Now she tried to back away. "Have a good life, Diego. And be proud of all you've accomplished."

"That sounds like goodbye." Her hair fell around her face in loose waves. Diego wrapped a one of his clean fingers around the deep red lock. "And I don't want you to go."

Penny smiled, the shadow in her eyes sad. "I can't imagine that we'll run into each other."

"Well *I* imagine that we'll see each other regularly when you're installing our garden."

"Really?" Her smile blossomed over her face, lighting her up from the inside. "That's great."

But she still wasn't coming closer. And then she shoved out her hand, practically poking him in the stomach, so he could…shake?

He took her palm gently in his. And she squeezed hard.

He hummed a little at the pressure on his bruised knuckles.

"Oh." Penny let go, then ran her finger over his knuckles. "What happened?"

"I expressed my displeasure."

"Hmm, well then, I guess I should be happy you aren't displeased with me."

"Far from it."

He tried to ease closer but she stepped back, all business. "I've got a contract with me if you want to look it over before you commit."

"Great." The last thing he wanted to talk about was contracts. Damn, he wanted to kiss her. Wrap her up in his arms and never let her go.

But her body language made that impractical. Even if he felt like touching her, holding her was necessary to his continued survival and happiness, she wasn't ready.

"Thank you, again." She was so stiff, so formal. He hated it. The casual carefree Penny he'd gotten reacquainted with over the past few days was gone. In her place was a stranger.

He leaned forward and kissed her cheek. "Thank *you*."

She practically jumped back. "Well, got to run."

She never even asked what he needed. If she had, he would have told her that he knew exactly what he needed.

Her.

SHE'D GOTTEN her first real client!

Elation bubbled through her like champagne. Not that she drank champagne. She was more of a beer girl.

She was going to do this. Her senior thesis project was going to become a reality. She couldn't be happier.

Penny ran toward the lodge. She couldn't wait to tell Meg. She rounded the corner, thinking she'd go in the back door to the industrial kitchen, and ran right into Jeffrey London.

"Oh, excuse me." She bent her head, not wanting to interact with him. She shut down like she always had right after the scandal with her parents.

But he grabbed her arm, stopping Penny in her tracks. His grip so tight she was going to have bruises. "You bitch."

"What?" Penny lifted her head. Gasped. Jeffrey London had a nasty purpling bruise along his jaw.

"First your family stole my mother's money."

So that's why he was so angry. One of her parents' victims.

"Then you destroyed my merger."

"I'm guessing you destroyed it yourself." Penny broke away from his hold. And this time she wasn't going to back down. "Maybe if you'd take a break and enjoy nature, you'd be happier."

"You aren't worth my time."

Weird. The words should hurt but she couldn't get over that bruise. "Did Diego punch you?" She thought about his swelling knuckles.

London's face turned an unhealthy shade of red. He stomped off without answering.

Just because Diego had called off their merger didn't necessarily mean anything. He hadn't defended her, he hadn't stuck up for her. Even so, a curious seed of hope unfurled inside her.

OPERATION SUCCESS WAS A GO. Diego was ready to wow Penny at the final camp retreat event.

All the CAR employees were here. Zin was set up on an

elevated platform like a queen on a throne so she could survey the kitchen.

"Okay, everyone!" Zin yelled into her megaphone. "Time for the cook-off!"

She was far too damn happy. "Tone it down."

"Can't." She grinned from her perch on the edge of the folding table. "I'm excited."

"About what?" Diego groused.

"I always wanted a sister."

"Zin, I've got a long way to go before Penny will be anything near sister status."

She beamed. "You'll pull it off. I have faith in you."

"You're the only one," Raul muttered.

She cuffed him on the head.

Penny had just edged inside the door of the conference center's industrial kitchen. He was reminded of the first night at the cocktail party. She was flushed, her hair in braids, wearing a short, floaty floral dress and old Converse, yet she still managed to look ethereal. But the expression on her face was indecipherable.

An unwelcome flutter took up in his stomach. Not the near-constant grinding of the last year. But something far more worrisome. What if she turned him down? What if he never got the chance to ask?

And what if he nutted up and put his plan in motion?

"Everyone remember to mark off the final squares on your bingo card tonight! We'll be drawing names for prizes at breakfast tomorrow morning before we head home."

The last official event was the cook off. He'd made sure that Penny was going to be here by requesting her presence through Tegan.

"I've got our teams." Zin rattled off pairs of Diego's employees and they grouped together at one end of the giant island.

London, Sherry and the rest of his employees were conspicuously absent. They'd left the camp not long after Diego had proclaimed the merger was dead.

"Diego and Penny."

Penny jerked. Her gaze met his, but the hurt that he expected to see was masked with a bland, blank gaze. He had no idea what she was thinking right now. Protecting herself. From him.

He couldn't remember the last time he'd been this nervous.

"Okay, everyone has ingredients in front of them. You've got thirty minutes to come up with the best camp burger ever. And...go!"

Penny took her time coming over to Diego. "So what's your idea?"

For a minute, he thought she meant his plan to apologize and get her back. Or get her. Depending on your point of view.

"I'm hoping we can come up with a plan together."

Penny avoided his gaze.

"I'm surprised you're still here," he couldn't help but comment.

"I promised Michael Tully I'd stay." *Or I would be out of here* was pretty much implied.

Ouch, damn. He deserved that.

"Okay." He blew out a breath, focused. "What are your favorite toppings?" Fortunately he already knew. He'd begged for mercy from Meg and she'd given him a little insight into Penny's favorites.

"Tomato."

"One Pretty Penny Farms beefsteak coming up." He placed the perfect tomato on the stainless steel counter.

She jerked.

"Butter lettuce."

He pulled out a head of her lettuce and set it next to the tomato.

"Caramelized sweet onions."

This one hadn't come from her farm. But he set a Vidalia onion next to her produce.

She blinked, studied their prep area but didn't say anything.

Next, he pulled out some adobo peppers.

"That didn't come from my farm." She raised an eyebrow.

"This is my contribution." He pulled out a jar of mayonnaise and set it next to the peppers. "I'm not so good with a knife." He handed the sharp chef's knife to her.

"You sure you want to hand an angry woman a knife, *mi hermano*?"

"Shut up, Zin." Diego rubbed his hands on his shirt. "Cut the onions while I form the patties?"

"Sure." While she chopped, he got the rest of the ingredients ready to go. She finished quickly.

Now or never. He dumped the meat in a stainless bowl, then pinched some sea salt. "Salt of the earth. That's you."

She still hadn't said much.

"Hold out your hand."

She cocked her head. He cupped her palm beneath his

and shook a bit of black pepper into her palm. "Spicy. That's me."

She just stared at him.

"Go ahead. Add it."

Penny dumped the pepper into the bowl but her hand wobbled for just a moment. Which gave him hope. Because her expression sure didn't.

The conversation swirled around them as his employees laughed and joked and had a great time.

She looked to be one step away from bolting.

"Fuck it." Diego tossed the bowl to the counter. This elaborate ploy to apologize with clever analogies and practiced lines wasn't going to work. It was easy to have a business plan but she needed passion and sincerity not a rehearsed proposal. As the bowl clanged on the counter, he took her hands. Around them the conversations halted. "I spent the last fifteen years saying the right thing, doing the right thing, and being cautious with every move."

Diego grabbed Penny by the waist and lifted her onto the counter. She yelped and clutched at his hands. "What are you doing?" she hissed.

"Being myself." He laughed. "Without rehearsal. But one thing remains the same."

"What?"

"You deserve a public apology."

"I don't need one."

"I think maybe you do."

Now everyone was staring at him, at *them*. "I'm sorry I was an ass."

"You mean you *are* an ass," she shot back.

And everyone laughed.

"Maybe. But I'm an honest ass." Diego stepped between her thighs. "I had this whole thing planned out. But that's not who I want to be anymore."

"Who do you want to be?"

He began to sweat. His stomach flipped, knowing this was his chance. And he couldn't afford to blow it.

"I don't want to be the guy who hurt you." He wanted to be her hero.

Her face softened, and she blinked her green eyes. "Too late for that."

"How about I won't hurt you again?"

She shrugged, looked down, not meeting his gaze.

Diego bent his forehead to hers, focused intently on Penny, filtering out the rest of the room.

"I want to be the man who makes you happy," he confessed softly. Because right now that was his goal. And he was fiercely goal oriented. He might have abandoned the plan, but the goal was still firmly rooted in place.

A glow of pleasure flushed her face and she ducked her head. "I doubt that's all you want."

He had to be honest. "No. I know you work hard at what you do. And I'd be bored waiting around while you work. Especially after working fifteen, sixteen hours a day for years."

"Okay." She wasn't turning him down. "What else?"

What else? What else? What had made him happy in the last few days? What if he were free to do anything he wanted? His heart began to beat erratically.

"I want to spend more time working on cars," Diego blurted out.

The dead silence began to dissipate. "What is he doing?"

was the most common murmur. Followed by, "Holy shit, he's quitting?"

"What about your merger?" Penny asked the question swirling in the growing furor.

"Yeah, well, that's a no-go." Diego lifted his gaze to encompass the entire crowd of his employees. "There will be no merger. I told Jeffrey London we don't have a deal."

A cheer went up from his employees.

"Did everyone think it was a bad idea but me?"

"You were blinded by achieving your goals," Penny said. "There's nothing wrong with having goals."

"Unless you pair up with assholes."

She threaded her fingers through his. "No argument from me."

Shit. She could be talking about him. But he soldiered forward. "And unless you lose sight of your dreams."

Penny smiled softly. "What are your dreams?"

"You." He squeezed her fingers, his palms unusually sweaty as he waited for her reaction.

He could hear the female sighs in the room. But the only one he wanted to sigh was Penny.

"That's really...sweet."

Sweet? That did not sound promising. He bent his head to hers, wanting a bit of privacy. "How about sexy?" he growled in her ear.

"Sexy too," she whispered back.

Diego wrapped his arms around her waist and bent in for a kiss to seal the deal.

"Stop!" Zin shoved something in between their bodies.

"What the hell, Zinnia?"

Zin waved the card in his face. "You've got to fill out your bingo card."

"I don't give a shit about bingo right now, Zin."

But Penny giggled. Her laugh still sounded like the trill of the birds, and he wanted to spend an eternity listening to her.

"You like to win." Zinnia stabbed her finger at the Free square in the center. Except it didn't say *Free* any more.

It said *Free Kiss*. All the other squares were filled in.

Diego looked at Penny. "You forgive me?"

"Yes."

"You willing to give us a try?"

"Yes."

He shoved the card back at Zin. "I already won."

EPILOGUE

The helicopter rotor *whomp-whomp-whomped* overhead.

Penny pressed her hands to her lower back and arched. She and Brad had spent the day in the fields along with her other workers harvesting the produce for tomorrow's farmers' market. Before, she would have been in the bath, and then heading to bed alone.

Now, she sipped her wine, waiting impatiently.

When she heard the rumble of an engine zooming up the driveway to her farmhouse, she opened the door with a huge smile. She leaned against the doorframe, wineglass in hand, one foot on top of the other. Diego strode toward her in khakis and a blue button-down. He grabbed her around the waist and lifted her up. The light was fading but his eyes were bright and happy in the soft porch light.

His smile still had the power to bring her to her knees. She wrapped her arms around his shoulders and held on, snuggling into the curve of his neck. His body was solid and

173

real and constant against hers. "How was your day?" She pressed kisses up the side of his throat.

"You're looking at the new proprietor of Ramos Repair and Restoration." The empty garage at the edge of town was now his.

"You excited?"

"Yes. I handed over the day-to-day control to Raul this morning." Diego laughed, the sound a rumble against her mouth, before he kissed her silly.

He finally accepted that he hadn't been happy for a while. While he'd still be on the board of his company, he wanted to work with his hands again. And it turned out his cousin loved running the company.

Jeffrey London ended up not challenging the merger contract breakdown. Right now, he was embroiled in a pretty ugly divorce, and three of his former assistants had filed a sexual harassment suit against him.

After the fallout with London Automotive, Diego had discussed other ways to take Ramos CAR to the next level with the Breakfast Club and come up with another solution.

"With the release of the end-user app that Peter designed, we should hit billion-dollar valuation this month." The beauty of the app was they didn't need to add a significant number of employees and Peter had done the work for a percentage of the profits.

"Congratulations."

"We'll have to celebrate later." His suggestive tone caused her belly to flutter.

She reached in the fridge and grabbed a bottle of local craft beer. "How's your stomach?"

"It's fine." He smiled and brushed a lock of hair from her face.

The ulcer he had developed while working on the merger was mostly under control now, but Penny still couldn't stifle the need to take care of him.

Penny handed him the beer. "Guess what?"

He grabbed her around the waist and hugged her closer. "What?"

"Next week when you head to Boston, I need to hitch a ride." A deep satisfaction filled her. "I've got two new clients, a presentation to a major hospital group, and Duke and I are going to sit down and flesh out a bigger marketing plan."

He put down his beer, and took her wineglass from her, setting it carefully on the scarred farmhouse table.

"Nice."

She could hear the jealousy in his voice. "Don't worry about Duke."

Diego scooped her up into his arms and carried her toward the bedroom. "Why's that?"

"I don't want anyone but you." Penny kissed him softly. "I love *you*."

He tossed her onto the bed. She bounced and then he landed on top of her. "I love you too."

There were so many points where their relationship could have gone downhill. Combining households had been interesting. Diego moving part-time to the country was a huge adjustment for a city boy. And for Penny, becoming Diego's plus-one meant dressing up and going back into the society she'd shunned when she moved to western Mass and become a farmer.

But having someone to share her day with and wake up to in the morning had made all the difference in the world.

"You know what this means?"

"Hmm?" She didn't really care. As long as he loved her, life was perfect.

"My life is no longer semi-charmed."

Wait, what?

"It's all the way charmed."

Oh, she melted. "Mine, too."

Because love was the best fortune of all.

THANK you so much for reading Penny and Diego's story! I had so much fun playing in the Camp Firefly Falls world while introducing everyone to the Billionaire Breakfast Club.

Want to know what happens between D'Andre and his reporter? He's got a secret and she's the dead last woman he should hook up with…. One click EVERYTHING HE WANTS Book number 2 in the Billionaire Breakfast Club!

If you did enjoy this novel, below are a few ways you can help a writer out!!

Good: Lend the book to a friend

Better: Recommend the book to your friends

Best: Leave a review at Amazon, BN, iBooks, Kobo, Google Play, Goodreads...basically any place they sell or review eBooks. Every review helps my work get out to other readers and I cannot even express how much it means to me when you let people know you liked my work. Readers have so many choices nowadays and limited dollars to spend. It can be difficult to take a chance on a new author even if the premise sounds appealing. By reviewing books, you give other readers insight into the story world and help them make informed purchases.

THANK YOU, thank you, thank you for your support!!

P.S. Would you like to know when my next book is available? You can sign up for my new release email list/newsletter at Lisa's Confidants I send out newsletters once a month typically filled with info on upcoming books, friend freebies, and contests I'm involved in. I will never sell or distribute your email to other people.

ACKNOWLEDGMENTS

I had so much fun writing this story!!

First off, thank you so much to Gwen Hayes and Zoe York for starting the Camp Firefly Falls series last summer and allowing me to participate in season two. I was honored to be chosen.

Even though this is set at camp, this is the first book in my Billionaire Breakfast Club series.

Thanks to Sarah Hansen at Okay Creations for the beautiful cover. I seriously love it!!

Again my usual suspects, Adrienne Bell and LGC Smith for reading and general encouragement and coffee clutches and support.

Deb Nemeth, my wonderful editor who put up with multiple delays on our last two projects. I'm getting my sh*t together. I swear!

And to my family for just being awesome.

I've been finalizing this story in the middle of getting

ready to move and dealing with the myriad of details that go along with selling a house and moving three thousand miles away. But in more fun news, I will be super close to our fictional camp by Fall 2017. The Berkshires are lovely if you ever have a chance to visit. Thank you for reading!!

EXCERPT FROM EVERYTHING
HE WANTS

D'Andre Smith had it all.

Fame. Money. Women. On the outside, his life looked fucking perfect.

And if it wasn't, no way would he admit it to anyone. He flipped back the cuff on his hand-tailored Italian dress shirt, the cotton softer than the toilet paper he'd used as a kid, and checked the time on his Cartier Calibre watch. The reporter (how had he let himself get roped into that?) wasn't late. He was early.

He had a few minutes to go over his game plan for dealing with this interview. He hated the press. He kept his private life *private*. His pal Jay—Jason Hollingsworth IV for the society crowd—had insisted that D needed to start playing the media game to build buzz for the launch of his new company and its extremely important product, the concussion detection helmet.

Nonetheless, he'd still been tempted to bail on this interview. But Peter Nguyen, another friend from his sounding board, the BBC—Billionaire Breakfast Club—had agreed with Jay. So here he was waiting for a reporter, some prep school friend of Jay's, which was pretty much the only way he would agree to speak with the press. And when his momma found out, there was gonna be hell to pay.

Momma hated reporters. *Hated.* He wasn't fond of them either but after a particularly rough interview and story printed about her, Mary Smith had made him promise not to talk to them. He hadn't yet told her that he was going to have to break her cardinal rule.

The biggest problem with reporters was they always wanted to stick their nose in shit that was none of their business. As a result, he'd learned to dazzle and deflect like a pro.

He smiled at the hostess at Parker's Restaurant as she led him to his regular table in the formal dining room of the Omni Parker House Hotel in downtown Boston. His mother's favorite place. After the interview, he needed to meet with the catering director about his mother's fiftieth birthday party. It was going to be a surprise. And he wanted everything to be perfect.

Mary Smith deserved a banging party and he was going to make sure she got one.

Within a few seconds, the waiter placed sparkling water in front of him. "Your usual, Mr. Smith."

"Thanks, José."

"My pleasure, sir."

D pulled out his phone and clumsily texted his momma a good morning.

Predictably, his phone rang. "Hi, Momma."

"You know I don't like that texting. Why don't anyone just pick up a phone and call anymore?"

D'Andre sighed. "I didn't want to bother you."

"Talkin' to my baby boy is never a bother." She sniffed.

He was six four and two hundred seventy pounds, down thirty from his NFL career days, but to his mother he was still her baby.

"Thanks, Momma." His voice softened and his mouth curved. "Everything okay there?" He'd bought her the house in Brookline with his signing bonus ten years ago.

"The newfangled dishwasher is running rough."

"I'll get a repairman out there first thing."

"Thanks, baby."

"Anything for you," D'Andre said softly. His mother had sacrificed her best years to support him. Now it was his turn. "What's on your agenda for today?"

His mother kinda sounded like she was huffing and puffing. "Meeting some girls from church for an early birthday lunch."

A rustling behind him caught his ear and D turned around to see a stunning woman approaching his table.

Once during his rookie year in the NFL, he'd taken a hit so hard he'd been flat out on his back, the turf prickling his calves, breath clawing to escape his chest. The sky had swirled above him, a bright brilliant blue while he tried to remember who, and where, he was.

With one glance at this woman's dazzling ice blue eyes, his heart thunked in his chest and his head swirled, as if he'd taken a similar hit. That sensation of being flat out gobsmacked pummeled him just like that monster tackle from a three-hundred-fifty pound linebacker. He shook his head, trying to clear the sensation of having his bell rung.

Fuck him.

She wore a mannish navy suit with matching pointy flats. Not the least bit sexy. And yet he wanted to pull her into his embrace and hold on tight. A waterfall of straight platinum hair framed a stunning face of classic bone structure, bright blue eyes and a wide, unsmiling mouth.

"Mr. Smith." Not a question. Slightly haughty, frosty, ice princess.

He realized he'd been far too silent and his mother had been chattering away on the other end of the line.

"Well then, have a good lunch." He managed to finish his call without babbling like an idiot. He blindly pressed the end button. He guessed this was the reporter. She certainly didn't dress like a groupie.

That untouchable queen to peasant thing was really doing it for him. He'd never had this kind of physical reaction to a woman in his life. But he had to ignore it. Because her profession killed any possibility of engaging beyond this interview. Reporters were off-limits. For so, *so* many reasons.

So instead of asking her on a date, preferably one that started right here and ended upstairs in the Harvey Parker suite with both of them naked, he was going to ignore this insane attraction and do what he always did.

Flirt, distract, deflect, and get rid of her fast after he got his message across. He'd be out of here in thirty. He'd ignore his visceral reaction and get it done.

ABOUT LISA

USA Today Bestselling Author Lisa Hughey started writing romance in the fourth grade. That particular story involved a prince and an engagement. Now, she writes about strong heroines who are perfectly capable of rescuing themselves and the heroes who love both their strength and their vulnerability. She pens romances of all types—suspense, paranormal, and contemporary—but at their heart, all her books celebrate the power of love.

She lives in Cape Ann Massachusetts with her fabulously supportive husband and one somewhat grumpy cat.

Beach walks, hiking, and traveling are her favorite ways to pass the time when she isn't plotting new ways to get her characters to fall in love.

Lisa loves to hear from readers and has tons of places you can connect with her. It's a wonder she gets any writing done at all….

Be Lisa's Friend on Facebook

Sign Up for Lisa's Confidants
Visit Lisa on the Web
Follow Lisa on Pinterest
Follow Lisa on Instagram
Email Lisa
Be Lisa's Friend on Goodreads
Like Lisa on Facebook at Lisa Hughey Author

ALSO BY LISA HUGHEY

Black Cipher Files Romantic Suspense

The Encounter, A Prequel to Blowback

Blowback

Betrayals

Burned

Dangerous Game

Black Cipher Files Box Set (includes Blowback, Betrayals, and Burned)

Snow Creek Christmas

Love on Main Street: A Snow Creek Christmas – 7 Author anthology

One Silent Night (from Love on Main Street)

Miracle on Main Street (standalone novella)

Family Stone Romantic Suspense

Stone Cold Heart, (Jess, Family Stone #1)

Carved in Stone (Connor, Family Stone #2)

Heart of Stone (Riley, Family Stone #3)

Still the One (Jack, Family Stone #4)

Jar of Hearts (Keisha & Shane, Family Stone #5)

Queen of Hearts (Shelley, Family Stone #6)

Cold as Stone (John, Family Stone #7)

Family Stone Box Set (Stone Cold Heart, Carved in Stone, Heart of Stone, Still the One, & Jar of Hearts)

The Nostradamus Prophecies

View To A Kill #1

Never Say Never #2

ALIAS

Stalked (ALIAS #1)

Hunted (ALIAS #2)

Vanished (ALIAS #3)

Saved (ALIAS #3.5)

Deceived (ALIAS #4)

Billionaire Breakfast Club

His Semi-Charmed Life (Billionaire Breakfast Club #1)

Everything He Wants (Billionaire Breakfast Club #2)

She Feels Like Home (Billionaire Breakfast Club #3)

Coming July 2021 Sideways (Tracy's story!)

His Road To Paradise

His Dirty Little Secret

CPSIA information can be obtained
at www.ICGtesting.com
Printed in the USA
BVHW081222040521
606414BV00004B/419